A Suitable Brat

R. Cooper

A Suitable Brat

Copyright © 2025 by R. Cooper

All rights reserved.

No portion of this book may be reproduced in any form without written permission from the publisher or author, except as permitted by U.S. copyright law.

Cover art by Lyn Forester

Content tags: age difference, alcohol consumption, on-page sex, overstimulation, sex work mention, reference to freezing, frostbite, in-universe polyamory, possessiveness

Blessed

Copyright © 2023 by R. Cooper

All Rights Reserved

No portion of this book may be reproduced in any form without written permission from the publisher or author, except as permitted by U.S. copyright law.

Content tags: : a/b/o-universe tropes, including heats, canon polyamory and polygamy, self-image issues, character who often forgets to eat, on-page sex including multiple penetration

Contents

A Suitable Brat	1
Part One	2
Part Two	35
Epilogue	77
Blessed	91
Blessed - Part One	92
Blessed - Part Two	110
Blessed - Part Three	119
The Suitable 'Verse	144
Also by R .Cooper	145
About the author	146

A Suitable Brat

Part One

WESTIN CLOSED HIS EYES and inhaled deeply, exhaling moments later as he listened to the hum of conversation around him and the rattle of crockery from the direction of the kitchens. Steam from different fragrant teas drifted his way, mingling with the Maareshetal blend he'd chosen, the cress spice from his bath oils, and the wine enjoyed by someone at the table next to his. Laughter sounded from the direction of the inn's bar, rising high and then falling low enough to allow him to hear, or imagine he heard, the faint fall of rain on the roof high above him.

The rain was going to get worse, or so Westin's wrist insisted. The ache hadn't yet turned to pain, but it tugged at him, drawing his focus from the soothing, familiar sounds of Solace House.

An outguard's life was often one of discomfort. An old injury shouldn't rankle so much.

He shifted slightly in his chair and took another breath, counting slowly before he released it. Maareshetal teas were too bitter for some, but that was only when consumed too quickly. Boiling water was poured over the leaves, and then they were supposed to sit, the tea growing smoother as it cooled enough to be drinkable. That was why Westin had ordered it; to give himself the time to seek the peace that had so far eluded him.

Even his costly bath hadn't offered the sort of calm he'd expected. The rush of distant rain didn't seem to be doing much either.

Exasperated, Westin opened his eyes to stare at the teapot and cup on his table. There were some in the Outguard who found ways to calm themselves with activity, often fighting, but sometimes routine or mindless tasks: kit repair, chopping wood, even mucking stables.

Westin had no desire to do any of those things and, while Solace House was known to be accommodating, he doubted they wanted him messing about with the staff's assigned duties.

Any might feel conflicted in his place, he told himself, then sighed and took a sip of his tea, though it was too early for it to be enjoyable. Perhaps he'd spend the money and get a different tea, something less fussy and more easily consumed.

He glanced around although he had already looked the place over for trouble a few times, an Outguard habit that might stay with him even once that life was behind him.

He gave one of the open booths a frown it didn't deserve, then moved his gaze up to the high ceiling above the main floor of Solace House, then back down to where food and drink were offered at the many tables or in the booths that lined the walls. Chandeliers kept the room bright despite the darkness of the rainy evening, illuminating the bar and the door to the kitchens, the wide, welcoming entranceway, and the stairs leading to the rest of the inn.

Solace House occupied a strange space. A day's ride or a few hours by boat outside the capital and situated near enough to the river to lure all manner of travelers, it was considered by most to be under the jurisdiction of the current ruler, like the capital itself. However, it actually stood on the border of two territories, not including that of the capital, although the powerful noble family who governed the larger of the territories seemed to have no interest in fighting over the strip of riverfront land or in claiming the rents from the inn.

That could change of course, beat-of-fours being how they were. But the smaller noble family with the better claim was a peaceable one, and since the patch of land wasn't suited to farming, the more powerful beat-of-fours likely didn't consider it worth fighting over. Or perhaps they pitied the smaller, weaker Corilyeth, as much as nobles could pity one another once ambition got involved.

Over centuries, the Corilyeth had been leveled by opportunistic rulers and their territories reduced. The landlords of Solace House they might be, but they were wise enough to leave the inn alone and to be generous to the owners, letting them run it as they saw fit and not collecting any rent.

The owners of Solace House had put that money right back into their inn, earning it quite the reputation. Visitors could ride from the capital or stop for the night on their way in or out of the city. Some went out of their way to do so, or to journey from farther territories specifically to spend time in the inn where the chandeliers and lit windows promised warmth, comfort, and, of course, solace.

Solace meant something different to each visitor. Solace House offered nicer beds than most inns. Nicer food, nicer drink. More varieties of tea or wine. One could visit to have a pot of tea or a meal, or to spend the night, or to spend several weeks. There were also hot baths, with an array of luxurious soaps and oils on offer. But of course, the main draw of Solace House was the conversation.

Conversation in Solace House could mean talk or it could be a polite phrase for whatever the customer was truly interested in.

To be fair, that was often still talking. Or really, someone to listen. At tables, or behind curtains in the booths on cushioned bench seats, or even upstairs if someone paid for a room. Talking, with someone to truly listen, *was* the desired activity for many, at least according to Hely, which Westin could believe. Many people, in this inn or out of it, were desperate for company and for someone to listen to them. Sometimes, that meant spilling their problems to outguards. Outguards, in turn, then needed someone to listen as well, and many of his friends in the guard seemed to view Westin as a reliable conversation partner. A comfort and a good listener.

Westin didn't mind. But he appreciated that the workers at Solace were paid and paid well to do so because listening could take a lot.

Of course, some customers came to Solace and wanted other forms of peace or comfort, or perhaps not comfort at all. But that was up to the worker and rarely happened on a customer's first visit.

Paid friendship, some might call what was offered. Some wanted company, and someone to listen, and perhaps touch, whatever that entailed. Some found that within Solace House, though many found that with friends, as outguards often did, for much of an outguard's time was spent alone or with strangers, and friends encountered on the road or in the capital were a great source of such companionship. At least, so it was for many.

Westin took another sip of his tea and realized he'd missed the moment it would taste the best. But since it was still drinkable, he had some more. He had no call to be sighing over some tea. He was in a warm, bright room, surrounded by people who were trying desperately to shed their troubles for a few hours. He'd had a wonderful bath, and a decent cup of tea, and might get a good night's sleep since he'd paid for a room. He could have pressed on despite the rain and reached the capital tonight. The palace guards would let in an outguard no matter the hour, although in truth, it would be so late by then that it would almost be morning.

And... a night of hard travel hadn't suited him. Not anymore. Not if he didn't have to. He'd rather be warm, and the bath had seen to that.

Yet, with that problem resolved, his mind still could not settle.

He hadn't wanted to reach the capital, that was the truth of the matter. Though he'd only bought himself a day. A night and a day to reconcile what he wanted with what he must do. Perhaps another day if the rain turned to storms that would slow traffic along the river. Westin's aching wrist said that was a possibility, and he shivered at the idea of traveling in cold, driving autumn rain.

Westin was old for an outguard. Over forty years reached was about the age to realize that wandering the country in every kind of weather, under every kind of condition, was no longer worth the pay. Most his age settled into the barracks to teach, or had already left the Outguard years before, or retired to serve a noble family known to be kind.

"You waited too long," Hely observed in his familiar, calm tone, touching Westin's shoulder as he passed him on his way back to the bar or the kitchens. "Your tea won't be good. I'll bring you a new pot."

"No need to bother. It's fine as it is," Westin called after him, watching Hely step behind the bar with the confidence of someone who called Solace House home.

A visitor at another table swung a look in Westin's direction, probably for his raised voice because Solace House was not a rowdy place, or possibly because Westin was slightly underdressed in just a shirt and trousers after his bath; no sign of the travel cloak or heavy cloth gambeson that most outguards wore for protection and to identify them to anyone in need of help.

But the visitor continued to stare, and Westin briefly wished for his cloak and armor back, only to wonder just what was wrong with him if he was already so unsure of himself. Twenty years in the Outguard and he'd forgotten how to simply exist in an inn as himself. Or perhaps something of the Outguard remained in his manner or his weather-roughened face, and the visitor had something they wanted to share.

Westin didn't know whether to sigh over that or invite them over. He wasn't retired, not yet, but he was already looking for problems to solve like a bored former guard who needed something to occupy their time. That was likely also why Hely kept glancing his way; he wasn't used to seeing Westin unsettled.

Westin tried to give the visitor a reassuring nod so they would resume their conversation with the worker sharing their table, then reached up to check that his braid at least passed muster for the common room. His hair was still damp from his bath but soft and as perfumed as a spice cake. He couldn't bring himself to enjoy the honeyed or floral scents in the baths, but the spiced ones were at least interesting.

The end of the braid fell between his shoulder blades, hair longer than most in the Outguard would bother with but not unheard of, and was dark as night if one ignored the streaks of silver. The rest of him, his plainer clothing aside, should have been acceptable. His broad brow, dark eyebrows, even his beaky nose, big though it was, were unobjectionable. He'd shaved his beard in expectation of returning to the capital and because he'd never cared much for the beards grown while traveling, though they were certainly easier to deal with than trying to shave on the road.

The skin of his jaw was smooth as well, the work of more potions from the baths. He ought to buy some before he left. Solace House did offer them for purchase, and who knew when Westin might make it back this way. And perhaps once at home, he'd want to look his best.

Even with no one but family to show off for.

Westin turned away from the visitor to have more tea, although the visitor continued to eye him. They looked wealthy. Maybe they were the kind of beat-of-four to object to Westin's simple clothing. The wool of Westin's shirt was decently woven and undyed, a pale off-white that went well with his dark, gold-under-brown coloring, the collar loose and untied because Westin was still warm from the bath. The bit of chest hair peeking out shouldn't have offended anyone, and Westin wasn't remarkable enough in any direction to attract that much attention. Maybe the visitor had seen Westin arrive, and Westin, tired from travel and a few nights of poor sleep, had walked with less care than he should have.

He thought he walked quite well for a man missing a few toes, though that had taken time and effort. But he did grow clumsier when exhausted, and some people were strange about those with injuries or difficulties.

Then Tura, the worker sitting with the visitor, turned around and said with a smile but loud enough for Westin to hear, "That's Westin. He doesn't work here," before taking the visitor's hand in his, which effectively recaptured all of their attention.

Westin blinked several times and resisted the urge to glance to Hely. Hely knew everything anyway and would hear about it from Tura by morning. Nonetheless, Westin focused on sipping his tea and considering if he had 'good listener' written somewhere on him.

It was that, or the gray in his hair, or his size. Those could attract people. Westin wasn't all that large—not among outguards anyway, who tended to be broad and tall. Being a giant wasn't a requirement, but the hazards of the work were reduced for those who looked at first glance as though they would win all fights. Smaller outguards traveling alone certainly seemed to get into more trouble.

The ache in Westin's wrist spiked, nearly making him drop his cup, and he glanced up as though he could peer through the roof to the clouds.

"Are you in pain?" Hely's question arrived a blink before Hely did, setting a new pot of tea on the table before seating himself at the chair on Westin's right.

"You're too good at your job." Westin informed him without malice.

"Observation is something they teach outguards too," Hely said, not appearing even a tiny bit modest. "But I *am* very good at my job, yes."

One of the best, if the stories were true, although these days, Hely really did stay mostly behind the bar or work managing the inn. He might still have regular customers, or friends, or those who were both, but keeping things running smoothly seemed to make him happier.

There was a thought; Hely had changed a career, or at least, changed how he handled it. Westin ought to consider that.

He glanced over Hely instead, his short hair, also showing gray, his big green eyes, the nearly spotless apron.

"Are you all right?" Westin wondered. "Still enjoying life away from customers?"

"It's not about me." Hely smiled. "Not out in the common room like this. Tsk."

Westin had not put conversation on his tab and gave Hely another look. "I haven't asked for that."

"You're not happy." Hely reached out to accept the cup of wine one of the workers brought over for him. "Usually some rest, a bath, tea or a meal, and you're at least settled. Tonight, you're almost twitching. You never twitch, not our Westin. Perhaps what you're looking for is not to be found in Solace House."

He managed to sound a little insulted.

"It might not be anywhere," Westin answered, then hurried on when Hely's eyes widened. "If you want to be off your feet, I don't mind. But I truly didn't come here to complain to you. You're busy as it is. Unless," Westin paused, "*you* had something you wanted to talk about?"

"Westin." Hely had some wine. "Don't you do that enough? Offer to listen? And for free?" He had some more wine, or at least, *appeared* to have some wine. Westin had long suspected most of the workers in Solace House didn't actually drink much wine or ale while working.

He rolled his eyes at Hely's concern but softened it with a smile. "I don't mind most of the time." Which was true. "Especially not with friends."

Hely grinned for that, a real one that crinkled the corners of his eyes. His husband adored those crinkles.

But they were there and gone; Hely was serious again. "But do they listen to you, your friends? When the other outguards find you to share a campfire, or turn to you for an ear or a body, do they also allow you to do the same?"

Westin regretted ordering tea. Wine suddenly seemed a much better idea. "That's a little more pain than I was looking for this evening," he said lightly.

"What are you looking for?" Hely raised a politely questioning eyebrow. "You aren't here to sit in silence—you're frowning. Which is in itself an event. Our patient giant is frowning." Westin wasn't a giant but didn't bother interrupting Hely. "Either an injury is troubling you or you have a problem. You're going to end up brooding. You're nearly there now. I refuse to allow it. You're my friend and a good customer, but also," he leaned forward and lowered his voice, "it will affect the mood in here."

Westin cracked a smile despite himself. Hely seemed pleased with that result, leaning back again.

"I'll tell you what I'd tell anyone who'd want me to be direct: think about what it is you're actually looking for." Hely left the options—peace, companionship, quiet, excitement, touch, a fuck—unspoken. "And then consider where that might be found and if it's here. If you need further help, then I would ask if you want to be happy or if you want to be content, and when was the last time you were either."

Summer. Westin had last been happy in late summer, with autumn in the air but the weather still warm enough to make him sticky beneath his clothes and stare longingly toward the river parallel to the road he'd been on. He should have hurried to get to the next village, not let his gaze linger on the sparkling water so often that his desire to jump in and cool off had become obvious.

No, Westin thought in the next moment. *Not then. Later.* In that village that same evening, in a too-small room, in a too-small bed, sticky and hot all over again. A barn would have done for a bedroom. Nobles and innkeepers were required to give outguards somewhere to sleep, and piles of straw happened more than straw-stuffed mattresses. But Sun had insisted on a bed.

"I don't think I'll find that here," Westin realized aloud. Nor was he likely to find it in the capital or anywhere else. He might have told himself that he hadn't yet made up his mind about retirement, but he had and that memory proved it. He had felt heavy even then, as if a part of him had known it was his last trip to that village, his last break from duty to slip his feet into a cool stream, his last time spent watching the brat charm an innkeeper into giving him something nice for less money or for free. He'd felt it in his chest then and he felt it now. He summoned a smile for Hely anyway. "But I'll settle for some peace if I can find it."

The entrance door opened with a crash of thunder, the suddenly louder sound of heavy rain, and the startled exclamation of someone at the bar. The rain was muffled again following the quick rush to close the door. Then thunder boomed with enough force to rattle dishes and Westin glimpsed a flash through a window—lightning, and not that far away, before another rumble passed over the inn.

"Just in time," the new arrival panted a few feet from the threshold, a long, hooded cloak dripping a puddle at their feet. The dark wool was familiar, practical and sturdy and meant for nights like this one. Hanging from one of the visitor's hands was a bundled travel pack, and in the other was a sword, still in its scabbard and gripped around the middle—to be carried, not to be used.

"The fae and their mothers bless it all," the newcomer swore—not too loudly, in all fairness, but the common room had gone silent at his entrance, so the words traveled "Not a night for anyone to be out."

The cloak was almost too large for what seemed a slender and not especially tall figure The hood fell to below the fellow's nose, keeping most of him hidden until he pulled the hood back, baring his handsome face to the gazes of everyone in the common room who hadn't returned to their conversations.

Some of those conversations seemed to die again, unless Westin imagined it. He didn't believe he did.

A worker fluttered over, ostensibly to take the wet, dripping cloak before it could do more damage to the floor, but there was likely some interest there as well. She certainly took her time explaining herself and helping with the clasp at the newcomer's throat.

It was good that she did so, Westin told himself. He had seen Sun shake off water like a dog—though, granted, Sun had been in the house of an unfriendly noble and the rudeness had been intentional.

"Blessed fae," Sun swore again, quieter but still audible some distance away at Westin's table. "Why does it smell like every good thing in the country in here?" It was nearly a sigh. "Roasted meat and baking bread from one direction. Then jasmine and roses. Or lilies? Light and sweet as a noble's bathwater? Is that scent you? What a lovely choice." He sniffed the air, possibly to amuse the worker practically giggling for him. "Roses and violets," he finally determined, which drew another giggle from the worker. Apparently, Sun had guessed correctly.

Hely made a small noise. Westin assumed it was because the worker was younger and new and had forgotten that she was supposed to be charming customers, not the other way around.

Well, at least with unknown customers, they were supposed to be charming. After all, some customers didn't come here for *charming*. And Sun was an unknown customer, as far as Westin knew. He certainly had never mentioned visiting Solace House. But then, Sun could be guarded. He might be a returning visitor and hadn't mentioned it to Westin because he didn't want Westin to know. But Sun tipped his head back to marvel at the high ceiling and the sparkling chandeliers as though he'd never seen them before, so Westin doubted he was a regular.

"Exactly as they say," he remarked with appreciation, his gaze skipping over to the stairs and what was visible of the two upper stories on the east wing of the building, then returning to the ceiling before falling to the wide bar and all the stools lined up for those who wanted a nice meal or a drink but no conversation.

The worker, perhaps having received a chiding look from Hely, disappeared with the wet cloak, leaving Sun on his own in front of the entrance, his hands full, his attention elsewhere. He appeared to be in good spirits and not noticeably injured. Westin found some comfort in that.

On the smaller side for an outguard, Sun reached Westin's chin, and appeared slender, perhaps even slight when without his gambeson—and even when with it, to be perfectly honest. That gave the impression that he was weak, which had fooled more than one drunken lout causing problems in a tavern. Sun, like most outguards, was all muscle from training and from days upon days spent walking or riding. It was not a life that allowed for much spare food, and in Sun's case, without any family to supplement his income, he was possibly ever slightly too thin. Something he'd resent Westin for suggesting but then wheedle Westin into buying meals for him without any space in between to consider any contradiction or hypocrisy.

He'd charge, "How dare you?" or "Fuck you," in one breath, and then stare enviously at Westin's plate until Westin pushed it toward him and got up to order more for himself. He had a warm smile for servers and grooms and library assistants, and a meaner one reserved for anyone who happened to have pissed him off. Both smiles suited his exceptionally handsome face, which he knew.

He had short, sleek, dark hair, starting to curl around his ears, and warm brown skin not weathered too much, either because he had only been an outguard for seven years, or because he wore his hood up when traveling in all but the hottest weather.

Westin suspected that was about the freckles that many an outguard had teased Sun for when Sun had been younger. The freckles, a starry sky across his nose and cheeks that spilled down to the top of his chest and even to the back of his neck, made Sun, already slender, already small, and, at the time, young, look even younger.

At not-quite eighteen, Sun had responded to the teasing with violence, leaping into fights he had often lost until he'd learned to fight better. Westin had heard about the conflicts before ever setting eyes on the Outguard's wolfling, as the others had called him. In time, Sun had calmed, learned to understand teasing and camaraderie, and taken the lessons of the guard elders to heart, but still, he worried over more freckles, and so the hood stayed up.

It wasn't the only area where the supposedly wild wolfling fussed over his appearance. He shaved regularly no matter where he was because his attempts to grow a beard hadn't gone well, and wore tightly fitted clothes in and out of the capital that showed off the muscles in his arms and legs and the firm curves of his ass.

Old Lim had taught the wolfling patience, and how to get along with others, and that diplomacy was easier than challenging the entire country. The former weapons master had helped to hone Sun's skills and make him a deadly creature. But Sun had learned how to dress and charm and present himself to win over others all on his own.

Westin had been an outguard for twenty years. He knew defenses when he saw them. He also knew not to poke at them. If Sun wanted to use his face and body to get what he needed, Westin was hardly going to challenge him about it. Anyway, Sun would probably laugh in his face if he tried, the biting, delighted laugh that put Westin in mind of sharp puppy teeth.

He'd last heard that laugh when he'd given in and left the road to follow Sun to the river, where Sun had already shed his clothes on the bank and vanished under the surface of the water.

Westin, far more cautious, had removed his boots and socks, rolled up his breeches, and sat on a higher portion of the riverbank to dangle his feet in the water. That was cooling enough for his dignity, and didn't involve air drying on a riverbank or trying to put his clothes back on while damp. They were due to reach a village and an inn that evening. He could bathe there.

Nearly the very moment his feet were in the water and Westin was sighing at the blissful feel of cold water on overheated skin, Sun had popped up between his knees, merry at getting Westin to join him without even a pretense of an argument first.

Sun had doubtlessly watched Westin yearn for the river and taken it upon himself to win a debate Westin hadn't known they were having. He'd directed his horse toward the river, slid from the saddle, and begun stripping his clothes off while Westin had watched like a mindless lump.

Once he'd won, getting Westin to the river and surprising him by starting up from the water, Sun had put his wet hands on Westin's knees, pushed his way between them, and laughed up at him with mean delight before sliding his hands higher still.

No one was that hungry for Westin that they'd lure him to the water specifically to get undressed and get their hands on him, but Westin knew better than to argue with the brat. And he hadn't wanted to, which Sun would have known.

If he hadn't, he certainly would have by the time Westin had drawn him up to kiss river water from his mouth.

"Another outguard?" Hely's voice pulled Westin from the memory. Hely seemed confused although not troubled; outguards probably were not frequent customers, not with Solace House being so close to the capital and the Outguard barracks, where a bed and a meal were free. "Did you invite him?"

Westin shook his head.

"Sun," he explained, watching Sun approach the bar and lean in to say something to the worker there. "Sunlark," he added.

"Sunlark?" Hely asked with real surprise. "That's a name for a horse, not a person."

Hely wasn't wrong. People tended to have names from the long-forgotten ancient tongue. Pets and working animals tended to have more fanciful names.

It wasn't Westin's place to share details, but Hely ought to know there were topics best avoided around the brat.

"His mother named him that while drunk, he says." It was all Sun ever said of his mother, except to sometimes joke, or not joke, that until then, people had simply called him "Child." He likewise shared no information about his father. Westin half suspected that Sun was part fae, but there were no obvious signs of it. Sun wasn't *that* little. And his hair, while a pretty color in the sun, was a normal human color. Sun either had no family or was ignoring the one he had, because instead of a family name, he identified himself as Sun of South Burrow, wherever that was.

That hair, currently curled around Sun's ear where he'd tucked it back while smiling at the bartender, was shining, although its gleam was nothing to the glitter of two ear cuffs high along the shell, or the darker cuff hanging from his ear lobe. There was, Westin belatedly realized, a slim cuff on one side of his nose as well. Except for the darker cuff, they were all polished silver. The darker one might have been pewter. One of them seemed to have agate or amber stones set in it that flickered in the candlelight.

Those were new.

Someone had been generous, Westin thought with a pain in his wrist and a faint ache in his chest.

"He's what? Half your age?" Hely guessed quietly. He wouldn't have missed how Westin was staring.

Westin tore his gaze away to blankly consider the far wall. He took a breath, then tried a smile. "Not quite that." His attention returned to Sun, who seemed amusingly taken aback by the selection the bar offered: ales, wines, and teas from all across the country, with no loyalty to any particular noble family, not even the one who controlled the land the inn was on. "Five or six years off from that," Westin added, then made himself turn to Hely and Hely's expression of patient interest. There was no judgment in Hely's tone, but there didn't need to be. "Though still far too old for him."

Hely met his stare levelly, evidently wanting Westin to know he was sincere. "I didn't say that."

Westin only sighed. That he was on the verge of retirement said enough. He poured himself a cup of tea and answered without tasting it.

"Too old for anything beyond what any outguards might do together," he amended. His future should be spoken of. "Hely, I plan to leave the—"

"There you are!" Sun called out, and Westin knew it was directed at him from both the flip in his chest and the reproach in Sun's tone. Westin had done something to vex the brat, which happened often and was rarely explained, although since the consequences mostly meant Sun teasing him, Westin had never fought hard for an explanation.

Sun moved with swift purpose, as if he intended to plant himself in Westin's lap despite the height of the chair and the table in his way. Sun hadn't once ever sat in Westin's lap in public despite acting as if he were entitled to; Westin was weaving fantasies with that summer day and his lonely future on his mind.

Sun was halfway to Westin's table when his gaze fell on Hely. His open-mouthed smile sharpened. His demeanor shifted from eager and excited to something altogether more calculated and worrying. Tura's customer tracked Sun's dangerous, deliberate progress until Tura clucked his tongue and left the table without a word of farewell. The customer, realizing his mistake, scrambled after him—too late, unless that was a game they played.

"Confidence works for your Sun," Hely remarked for only Westin to hear. He was watching the brat's approach as well.

Westin couldn't blame him. "Yes, it does."

"West," Sun showed his teeth in a different smile, "there you are."

Westin forced away the sliver of worry, or perhaps fear, at that smile and whether or not it was for Hely. "Is someone looking for me?"

Sun stopped. His hand tightened around the straps to his travel pack. "Lani said you often come here on your way to the capital." He didn't make it a question, but Westin heard it as one.

Sun glanced to Hely, then turned on his bright, charming attitude the way Westin had turned on the tap to the hot water for his expensive bath. Suddenly, Sun didn't look like someone who could be considered a walking armory of hidden weapons.

Westin normally approved of those weapons. The life of an outguard could be dangerous, and Sun was on the smaller side and needed extra protection. But he would prefer to avoid bloodshed in an inn known for peace.

"I do often stop here, yes," Westin said in the mild tone he used to end fights before they began. Perhaps Sun recognized it, because his eyebrows flew up. Then Westin, who ought to know better, who was certainly old enough to know not to poke wild creatures, couldn't resist adding, "Was there a desperate need for me?"

"*Westin*," Hely chastised, although Westin didn't dwell on what he'd done to deserve that tone. Not with the brat's cheeks flushing darker and his eyes wide and alarmed and pretty.

The surprise was only for a moment anyway. Then Sun fluttered his eyelashes and answered in an overly sweet voice, "You know you're irresistible to me, West."

Westin scoffed and shook his head. He was about to tease back in kind when Hely tapped the hand Westin had resting on the table.

Sun's gaze fell, possibly to Hely's hand over Westin's before Hely removed it to reach for his wine again. Then Sun was even more obnoxiously charming.

"And hello to you, handsome older stranger. You must be a friend of Westin's. He has so many friends."

"He's friendly," Hely agreed, smooth as cream.

Westin frowned between them, certain Hely didn't need a wolf pup chewing on his shoes, but uncertain if that was the case, or if Sun's flirting was genuine. It was hard to tell with Sun. The charming demeanor wasn't a lie, exactly, but he did definitely choose to put it on.

Westin finally cleared his throat to introduce them. "This is Hely, Sun. He works here. And yes, he is a friend."

For a moment, Sun looked at Westin as though Westin had just cheated at cards or stolen his horse. Then he was back to regarding Hely too warmly, too brightly. "I'm Sun. I would have said *I* was a friend until now."

Westin had his head back to retort when he realized he was being provoked. That was Sun. Always biting. Always testing. Never charming, not with Westin. But Westin had seen Sun grow into his skills over the years. Maybe Sun knew Westin wouldn't be fooled. Or maybe he just liked to bite certain people with a pup's needle teeth.

"Brat," Westin finally sighed, "you know you're my friend."

Evidently pleased with that despite being called a brat, Sun put his sword and his pack down, pulled a chair over to the table, and plopped down across from them. He raised his head to observe the room again as he removed his gloves and tucked them into his belt. "It really is a nice place," he said, and seemed sincere. "It's not the palace, but I've never thought of the palace as comfortable."

"Solace is for everyone," Hely remarked. Sun's attention slid back to him.

Westin spent yet another moment wondering if he was going to have to watch Sun flirt with Hely, but then Hely smiled coolly and Sun slouched in his seat, abandoning charm in favor of looking disgruntled to the point of sulky.

"It's still outside of my budget," he commented. He must have asked the bartender the prices.

"Surely not for food and a bath? Tea?" Hely offered, genuinely concerned but also making money for the inn, as was his job. "A drink? Many come here just for those, although not tonight in this weather."

Hely got another look from Sun. It wasn't warm this time, though. "Is that why West comes here?"

"You could ask me," Westin pointed out. He wasn't even spared a glance.

Hely continued to smile. "Let me know what you'd like, if you decide. I'll see what I can do for you."

Sun was not one to be put off with a smile. "As a friend of West's?"

"As a customer." Hely took, or pretended to take, another sip of wine. When Sun pushed out a growly breath, Hely added, "And yes, as his friend. He matters to me." He said that with weight. Westin would have said Hely was scolding but he didn't act like it and Sun only waited for him to go on without spiking up with temper. "And I don't think he'd want you to go without."

Sun swallowed and looked away. When he looked back—still at Hely, not at Westin—he grinned, bright and toothy. "He's generous."

Hely inclined his head as if a serious issue were being discussed. "*Too* generous, would you say?"

"Hey." Westin was hard to miss and yet they both seemed to have forgotten him.

Sun's eyebrows rose, then fell, staying down in a decidedly displeased manner that boded ill for someone. "I know of two guards who owe him money and who should have paid him back years ago but haven't."

"It's fine," Westin insisted. "Truly."

It got him a glance at least, scornful though it was. "They have the funds. You're too nice, West."

"Says the brat," Westin returned, taking a drink of his tea which once again was beyond its most flavorful point.

Sun gave Westin a sly, almost smug look. But silence from Hely made Westin tear his gaze away from a preening brat to look at his friend.

Hely's stare held *questions*.

Westin tried to think of why Hely should seem so startled, then realized he had just teased the brat... and called him a brat, for that matter. He suddenly felt the need to explain himself to Hely as if he were a new Solace House worker.

"The others sometimes call him that," he offered. Westin was a quiet, careful outguard and a respectful guest in all inns. Hely must think he'd lost his mind or had been at the wine. "It's meant fondly."

"It was not and they do not any longer." Sun punctuated that with another show of teeth disguised as a grin. "Only Westin calls me that now."

"Oh," Westin said again, warm with some shame. "I didn't realize it bothered you. I'll stop."

"Did I tell you to stop?" Sun scoffed to the ceiling, puffed out a breath, then gestured toward Hely. "Too nice." He gestured again. "Too generous."

He made no sense. Westin nearly gestured in appeal to Hely too. "*That* is why I still you call you that." He paused, but had no real fear of the knives up Sun's sleeves or in his boots or his belt or wherever else. "Brat."

He made the 't' especially crisp.

Sun lifted his chin and straightened his shoulders, but didn't have a single, snarling reaction to the nickname, though there was some color in his cheeks.

His blushes were subtle, but Westin had gotten into the habit of looking for them, even if he didn't always understand them. Sun could suck his cock on the bank of a river not far from a public road, but would flush ever so slightly darker when gently teased about his hair growing too long, or whenever someone—Westin—would buy him an extra cup of something or wait for him at a market stall while he debated which treat to get himself. The color looked good on him, made him seem youthful but not young. Excited, Westin supposed was a better way of describing it. Innocent or happy in a way Sun rarely got to be.

Hely coughed.

Abruptly aware that he was staring, *again*, Westin forced himself to look at Hely.

Hely was hiding behind his wine without drinking it. He arched an eyebrow.

Westin heaved a breath and gave in, admitting the truth with a nod.

"Well," Sun broke in as thunder sounded, "I could probably go for something to eat, judging from the delicious smells coming from the kitchens."

"And a hot bath," Westin added, firmly ignoring Hely, although aware Hely probably had both eyebrows raised now because Westin had nearly made that an order. Westin quickly tried to make it sound better. "You're wet and the night will be cold."

He was prepared for Sun to bristle. Anyone would have in his place.

Sun did stiffen, but then shook his head and leaned in. "I won't freeze, West." His tone was gentle. "But all right, I'll have a hot bath." He didn't glance down as if to look through the table to Westin's boots, and Westin's feet inside them with a shortage of toes, or in any way overtly acknowledge Westin's fears and the reasons for them. He was gentle, but that was all. Agreement out of the way, he inched in even further to sniff the air around Westin. "Can I choose perfume for the water too? I'll feel like a noble's pampered pet." His eyes were wide and breathtaking, dark enough to sparkle in candlelight. "Please?"

Westin had last seen Sun's eyes like that on a late summer's evening in an inn not far from a cool river.

"A room's better than a barn," he'd said, mischief in the smile he'd directed at Westin. The room hadn't cost a lot in the end; Sun had charmed the innkeeper too. *"Think of the sense of safety visitors will feel with two outguards nearby,"* he'd argued, getting the price knocked down within moments. Then he had stacked his things next to Westin's in a tiny room, by a tiny bed. Westin could have spent the night in a barn, which would have been free and where he would have had room to stretch out. Instead, he had pinned a gloating Sun to a sliver of a mattress and then slept restlessly in the heat with Sun passed out on top of him.

An uncomfortable night, Westin reminded himself, if a dear one.

He wasn't actually sure why Sun had requested the bed, except possibly to prove that he could. Sun probably got most of what he asked for from people, and Westin was no exception. But Westin had more money than Sun and he didn't really mind. Sun only ever asked for things like that from him anyway. Practical gifts. Certainly not jewelry.

"'Pampered pet,'" he echoed, gaze sliding to Sun's ear. The words flew out, quietly, if not sensibly. "I'm surprised there's no necklace or collar to go with those sparkles."

Blessed fae. It was not his business what Sun got up to when they were apart. It never had been.

A moment passed, Sun perhaps staring at him or perhaps frowning or perhaps considering getting up and leaving Westin at the table with Hely.

Then Sun slipped back into a slouch and reached up to stroke the cuffs at the shell of his ear. "You noticed." He smiled softly, possibly at the memory of receiving his gifts, and touched them again. "They *are* shiny, aren't they?" He turned his face toward Hely, but darted another look at Westin. "Do you think they suit me?"

"Oh yes," Hely agreed, calm, but then, he had no reason not to be calm. "You're a glittering, pretty thing even without them, and will likely only be more so after a bath and a meal have warmed you."

Sun shimmied at the praise before frowning delicately. "And the cost of those would be...?"

"Don't worry about it." Westin spoke without thought again, because he was an idiot. The idea of Sun in a bath in a real tub, with steaming, hot water and perfumes and soaps was distracting enough. The idea of Sun in such a bath while decorated with shining jewelry was apt to make anyone say foolish things. Westin blamed the knowledge that he would likely not see Sun much, or at all, once he retired. Sun wasn't even trying to charm him. Westin had no excuse for his behavior.

He picked up his cup of tea and downed it though it was cool and bordering on unpleasant. When he set the cup back down, it was to silence and two handsome men watching him with questions in their eyes.

"What? I'm not 'too generous' now?" Westin didn't snap. He was a patient giant, after all. He didn't even frown. Which was why he made himself add, almost pleasantly, "If you need a place to stash your pack and that sword, I have a room."

Westin didn't snap and he didn't angle. He made the offer to store Sun's belongings sincerely and Sun would know that. Sun would find his way to a room tonight almost certainly, and it very probably would not be Westin's. Westin was foolish at the moment, but he wasn't so foolish as to forget that.

"You got a room?" Sun prompted, voice rising. "For sleep or something other than sleep?" He glittered more than his many cuffs did as he turned to Hely. "That costs too, here, does it not? Or are the stories wrong?"

"Just a bed, Sun." Westin rubbed his wrist, irritable at the ache that meant the rain wasn't over, and that he was an aging man with injuries and pains, and all he had wanted to do, even in Solace House, was *sleep* in a nice, warm bed. "But if someone did decide to offer solace, even to me, what of it? The house has bills to pay, the same as everywhere else."

"'What of it?'" Sun was disbelieving then abruptly still and quiet. "'Solace?'" he echoed that too, young and lost, before his shoulders went back and his chin went up. "*Solace*," he said again. It was different the second time. "That means peace, right?"

"A nice bed's not jewelry, I admit," Westin insisted, somehow unsurprised when Hely nudged his foot as if to tell him to mind his tone. He pushed out a breath. "But I'm an old, tired guard. Perhaps we want different things."

Sun went still again, a slight line between his eyes. "*Old?*"

Hely cut in diplomatically. "A few hours of peace are worth a great deal to some at any age. Less so to others. But we try to make our friends happy here, as long as they *are* friends."

Westin couldn't tell if that was a warning or not, or why Hely thought he needed a warning. Westin already knew he was just another companion in the Outguard to Sun. He'd always known that. Some jewelry didn't make any difference, even if Westin was having trouble feeling settled this evening. But perhaps the warning, if there was one, was meant for Sun, who breathed hard and stared at Westin with an expression that could have been bewilderment, or anger, or anger about being bewildered.

But Sun was only a brat when it suited him to be. He was a well-trained, successful outguard the rest of the time. He smoothed whatever he felt from his face before he turned to Hely. His voice was even.

"What happens if someone isn't friendly?" he wondered, curious. "I didn't spot any burly types by the door as some taverns have."

Hely didn't seem offended. "Those get discovered and shown the door early on most of the time. One has to make friends here first. But it also helps that we have a frequent outguard visitor." He nodded toward Westin. Sun's gaze slid to him, lingered, then returned to Hely as Hely continued. "And though we are on Corilyeth territory and they aren't particularly strong, they are respected enough that locals mind their manners."

"It's other nobles that usually get pushy." Sun made a face. "Especially the lesser families." He paused. "Corilyeth? Four beats yet I've never heard of them."

"Their power has weakened over the centuries," Hely explained in an especially gentle voice. "I don't know all the history. But they don't charge us rent, and in return, we provide news from river travelers and we use their crops here in the kitchens. They are a farming family, known for that, and a little bit for their honey and some beets used for sugar."

"And Westin is a frequent visitor." Sun kept his focus on Hely. "Is he from around here, then? Westin Lyeth makes me think so. Not that he has ever said."

Westin opened, then closed, his mouth. "The family used to be Corialyeth," he heard himself offering a moment later, as though Sun cared for trivial bits of knowledge. "Five beats. But the family is so small now and their power so reduced, they dropped a beat a century ago so as to seem less foolish."

"So, you *are* a local," Sun interpreted. "Why not work here? Why the Outguard?"

Westin was unprepared for the intensity of the question, or for how Hely hummed and agreed.

"Yes. You would have done quite well here, Westin. Still would, more than likely. You have a soothing presence... most of the time, that is. There seem to be exceptions." Hely glanced pointedly at Sun.

Sun's mouth was set in a line. "But maybe too well. He'd listen and never volunteer a word about himself."

"I thought you liked that." Hely had finished his wine. Westin must have been wrong about how much the workers consumed. "All that attention on you must feel rather remarkable." Hely continued over the sound of Sun's small gasp, "You really would do well here, Westin. All it takes is discreetly determining what a customer is actually after. Some make it obvious." He gestured to Sun, who narrowed his eyes. "But with some it will take a few visits, or a few games of dice, or a few hours spent over tea discussing whatever you like. Most of our workers have regulars for that reason. It's less work once you know."

"Is Westin a regular?" Sun demanded immediately.

Hely smiled and ignored Sun to look over Westin's forgotten teapot. "It's barely warm now. Tsk."

"Warm enough to help you stop shivering." Westin met Sun's eyes right as Sun blinked, startled. "Even with your hood up, your hair got wet, and I bet some of your clothes as well. You've been trying not to show that you're cold." Westin didn't think about why. "But you are. Here. Before you get something hot." He poured a cupful and pushed it across the table at Sun. "There's a seat by the fire too, but I suppose you aren't done needling me yet."

Sun peered down at the cup, full of a flavor of tea he already might not have liked, but now no longer at its best, then closed both hands around the bowl of the cup and raised it to drink it all.

He made a face but swallowed, then returned the cup to the tray. "That was awful, West."

"Yet you drank it," Hely remarked.

"Appeasing my worries," Westin admitted stiffly. "I shouldn't make him do that, I know."

"*Make me.*" Sun scoffed. "I don't fucking think so. I choose, West. *I* do." He again turned to Hely, as if Hely was the only reasonable person at the table. "Understand, I knew people were messy before I was ever in the Outguard. They're horrible, just absolute shits. They reject others, or bully them, or treat them badly, and for the stupidest reasons—they *can* do all those things, I should say. Those same people will help an injured bird, or go out of their way to give water to travelers, or urge an outguard to go easy on a thief who was only after food. Makes no fucking sense, but they will. I didn't always see that. I was different when I was younger." He shot a heated look to Westin as though Westin had been going to object. Then he was back to talking only to Hely. "I see it more now, which is funny, with this work. Or not, I guess. Because outguards see far more of the country and the people in it than they might see in one little village. The majority of people are good *and* bad. And all of them have feelings that are a mess. They've all got quirks and fears and things that bother them. Even the ones who seem steady on the outside."

"And that's Westin?" Hely had not lost his softness.

"He's got fears and he has good reasons for them." Sun shrugged as if unconcerned but didn't meet Westin's eyes. "I don't need to be told to keep warm, but I don't mind if he worries. That's what you do with.... That's how you're supposed to do it, right? Accept that sort of thing with your person?"

He didn't say what 'it' was, but Hely nodded. "I'm so glad to have met you, Sun."

For a moment, Sun seemed younger, his chin dipping almost bashfully before he recovered, but by then, the blush had reached his cheeks.

"I'm glad you got to see more good in people." Westin was possibly softer than Hely had been.

Sun put his head down, then flicked a glance over to him. "Some people, no matter how much you push at them, are mostly *good*. It's like they work to be that way. If they can do that, then so can I, to be better and to be worth their time."

"They might not like being pushed," Hely pointed out.

Sun kept his gaze down. "It's not very peaceful, no."

"Too much peace can be boring." Westin was inviting more trouble for himself with that. It was nearly a dare, if he considered his history with Sun. But then, history was all there was now. So perhaps he wanted to dwell in it. Maybe that was why tea and the quiet of the common room hadn't helped him tonight. Westin would have peace enough when he left the Outguard, and that didn't seem to be what his heart longed for.

That felt like something he should have known before, and then like something he *had* known before, but hadn't needed to deal with because he'd see Sun every few months. As his mother said when referring to exceptionally good seasons: *sometimes* was better than *never*.

But never was approaching.

A strange moment for Westin to admit to himself exactly how much he liked being pushed, and proded, and nibbled on by sharp wolfing teeth. He really should have faced it before now. He had enjoyed it all, right from the start, from the very first time Sun had demanded his attention.

A friendly palace guard had thrown an impromptu party in one of the palace gardens to celebrate a coming baby, with everyone contributing their stashed casks or bottles and whatever food they'd wheedled the kitchen staff to make. Westin had acted as the judge of several card and dice games, then been drawn into some sort of game of chance with the Outguard's small danger, the rules of which he still didn't understand.

Their first real conversation. The first time Sun had needled and pressed on sore spots and then backed away. Assessing Westin, Westin realized now. But Sun must have approved of him, because he had approached Westin the following day and visited with him again the next time they were both in the capital.

Sun at that time hadn't been nearly as wild as the younger wolfling Westin had glimpsed once or twice when in the barracks, but he also hadn't been as close to settled as he was now. He'd been assigned to wander, unlike the guards who had regular routes, because those in charge had wanted him to see more of the country, and perhaps that had worked some to calm him.

Although Sun had just said it was that as much as it was meeting some of those who genuinely tried to be good.

He had no marks on his record that Westin knew of aside from those early fights, which Westin was willing to at least partly call self-defense. Sun was dutiful and well-liked, something Westin had glimpsed often enough when they'd traveled together.

Most of Westin's routes were regular, so he was easy enough to find. He worked alone, more because he didn't need assistance than a lack of desire for company, so he hadn't minded the brat popping up in places he was visiting.

Winding up in bed together, or on riverbanks, or alongside campfires, was common among outguards, even if Sun did poke and prod at Westin first instead of simply asking as most did. He could bare his teeth or smile prettily and bat his eyelashes, but it always ended the same, with the snarling wolfling flushed and lovely, voice rising with pleasure until he was full of cock, or had his seed splashed over his stomach and his hand working on Westin. Then his gaze was open and warm. Then he was pliable and clingy. Then he was hot hands and a shivering body and no desire to move out from under Westin even with an innkeeper banging on the door.

"He's more tired than I think he realizes."

Westin became aware that Hely and Sun were speaking, apparently about him. He blinked and tossed his head to return to the moment, but neither of them offered an explanation.

Hely was getting to his feet. "I was only visiting with a friend," he said to Sun, but then quirked a mischievous smile that would have done the brat proud. "Only visiting *for now*." Sun jerked in his seat, then glowered at Hely, who seemed unbothered. "I will order a bath to be readied for you. If you decide on food or a drink, please let me know. Or ask Westin to, since it seems he will be paying."

He didn't wink or give even a hint of a smile. He simply turned and made his way from the room.

Leaving Westin with an irritated brat who was practically throwing off sparks.

"I can see why you come here." Sun appeared to be speaking against his will. "He's good looking." This was pronounced matter-of-factly, but Sun was back to staring around the room instead of looking at Westin. "Everyone here seems to be," he added, before slinking down into his sulky posture and reaching up to stroke the cuffs on the shell of his ear. "Perhaps I'll have fun, then, while you look for *peace*."

Westin gritted his teeth. "*Sunlark.*"

It got him an unhappy look, so Westin reminded himself that it wasn't Sun's fault that Westin was older and tired.

He took a breath. "You never told me why you were seeking me out." If it was urgent, Sun would have said already, no matter how much he might have wanted to needle Westin by talking with Hely.

Sun examined his fingernails. "Did I say I was seeking you out?"

Westin swallowed the distant hurt of that and looked away to the flash of lightning through a window, only to look back at the glitter of the amber or agate in Sun's jewelry when Sun turned his head too.

"Westin!" Alit called as she cleaned off Tura's abandoned table. "Good to see you."

"It's good to see you!" Westin returned, feeling he was too loud with Sun so strangely quiet.

Sun watched Alit until she was gone. "Lani told me you might be here. *Apparently*, this a long-standing habit of yours." The weight he put on *apparently* made it significant, though Westin wasn't sure why. Sun carried on, his tone light, his expression almost furious. "Maybe I wanted to see the famed Solace House. It seems like a place where I could enjoy myself."

"It does." Westin had to agree on that whether he liked it or not. "But that's its purpose. Or at least, to offer rest and some peace."

Sun's scoff was barely audible. "'Peace' again."

"You don't want that? Even for a while?" Westin truly didn't understand, or believe, that. Not with his memories full of Sun clingy and sweet after a tup, a wild creature turned tame, content to be fed and petted and to sleep in someone's arms.

"That's what you want," Sun muttered, not quite under his breath. "Of course it is."

He pushed himself out of his chair without another word and went over to the bar, where the bartender seemed happy to see him again.

Westin absently rubbed his wrist though that wouldn't soothe the ache the rain had brought. Sun and the worker at the bar appeared to be discussing wines, not food, which Westin tried not to be vexed about, while also ignoring his own stomach's needs. Wines were poured, evidently for Sun to taste. Westin wondered if he or Sun was going to pay for that wine and suspected neither of them would. Sun and the bartender were enjoying themselves. Tasting wines from across the country in a warmly lit room while it stormed outside *was* peace to some. Westin shouldn't be jealous of that.

He shouldn't *be* jealous. He wasn't the kind. Though he hadn't avoided romance, he hadn't expected the lifelong love of his parents, and neither was he the sort to demand a one-and-only. He never had been.

Too generous, he imagined Sun sneering, as though not demanding love or a single lover was a failure and not something perfectly normal. Just because Westin didn't *demand* something didn't mean he couldn't accept it. Or so he argued with the Sun in his head. But the fact of the matter was, Westin wasn't territorial.

At least, he never had been. There was no point in such feelings. Some might even have said such feelings were dangerous. People like that started fights or wars, and often lost them. Ambitions, even for a single, devoted lover, were simply not something Westin had.

The Sun in his head bared his teeth before laughing at him, perhaps because Westin was watching Sun flirt while gifts from other lovers or friends twinkled at his ears, and Westin did not like it.

It was knowing this was all over, Westin told himself, as if that would cool the fire burning low inside him. He was upset because now Sun's flirting mattered more since it wouldn't be followed by time with Sun in the future. That was all. Westin hadn't actually *believed* Sun was here for him, although he and Sun had agreed to meet at the barracks in a few days. A visit before winter, when traveling was more difficult and even Sun wasn't going to want to track down Westin wherever he was and keep him company.

A small, hateful part of Westin wondered if that was why the winters seemed to have grown longer and harder for him in recent years. The larger, sensible part of Westin knew it was why Westin had stopped here instead of hurrying on to meet Sun a day sooner; he was going to have to tell Sun that he was leaving, and while Sun would be upset, he wouldn't be nearly as upset as Westin was at the thought of never, or hardly ever, seeing him again.

Westin was far too old to be this stupid about his own feelings.

Too generous, he imagined Sun *and* Hely telling him. Hely would likely add something about how conversation was important, and Westin ought to have more of them, instead of merely listening as others talked.

A glass goblet full of red wine appeared before him. Sun set it on the table in front of Westin when Westin didn't take it, then sat in the same chair he'd used before, but seated sideways so they weren't facing each other. "Min behind the bar swears that this should be to your tastes, although he also said you usually only get tea. I've seen you have wine elsewhere, which I told him, so he chose that one for you. I also ordered more tea for you since you gave me yours. But not that blend." He wrinkled his nose. "That was awful."

"It's good when you have it at just the right moment," Westin heard himself explaining, then abandoned his point to lean over and sniff his wine. "Spicy, not sweet," he murmured appreciatively, knowing Sun preferred sweet wines. "Thank you."

"I can be mannerly." Sun huffed. "Even if I'm no Hely."

Westin paused before he could raise the glass. "Why should you be Hely?"

Sun gave a snort. "Why indeed?"

Westin pushed the wine toward him, nudging the tray of old tea out of the way first. Sun gave him a look, but picked up the wine to take a swallow. He grimaced, but had another sip before he pushed it back.

Westin had a taste as well then, the rim of the glass warm from Sun's mouth although he wasn't thinking about it. They'd kept this wine in oak and he sighed appreciatively for Sun to hear.

"It's a good choice for me. Thank you again. But I get the sense that something is bothering you, brat."

He used the nickname gently but purposefully, and wasn't surprised when it made Sun turn to look at him. He also expected Sun to respond with a snippy retort, but if Sun had one, he kept it to himself.

"They pay people to listen here, don't they?" He didn't wait for an answer. "Do you?" Sun watched Westin hesitate and narrowed his eyes. But instead of a snarled or snappish opinion about that, Sun stayed serious. "Yet you're asking about *me*?"

Westin cocked his head to the side and frowned a little, trying to understand the heat beneath the question. Most of the chats Westin had with other outguards involved him listening. He was quiet, and people assumed that *quiet* equaled *wise*. Or perhaps they didn't think about it that much, or quiet was all they needed. But outguards spent their time investigating misdeeds or alleged misdeeds, or spying on nobles committing misdeeds. That meant they had burdens, and Westin didn't mind helping others carry theirs.

"You're my friend," he finally answered. "I can listen."

Sun's brows came together over his wounded eyes. "So can I."

Westin shook his head. "Of course you can. I didn't mean to imply you couldn't."

"Stop being nice." Sun worked his jaw. "This is a place to find peace or comfort, right? So which did you come here for?"

As he asked, his gaze left Westin to track something cross the room. Westin turned to see Hely paused in some errand to chat with someone at another table.

"You came here searching for peace," Sun announced, certain.

Westin exhaled heavily. "I am here because I had to make a decision. No, that's not true. I'm here because I made a decision, but I wasn't happy about it. And perhaps because I wanted to delay my arrival to the capital."

Sun pulled his attention from Hely to study Westin, his spine rigid and his hands pressed hard to the tabletop.

"So it's true?" he demanded. The heat was no longer under his words but a part of them.

Westin put out a hand to calm him without even knowing why he was upset. "What is?"

Sun took a shaky breath. "Weapons Master Chaus said you've been considering leaving the Outguard at last."

Westin felt like a small, old fool at the hurt and fury in Sun's eyes.

He swallowed, but in the end had to speak around the tension locking his throat. "I'm old for a guard, Sun. Winters are getting harder. Most leave by my age, or are thinking about it. You're young, but you'll see one day."

"You're leaving." Sun's tone was flat but his eyes said enough. "To do what? Oh." He glanced around without focusing on any one thing. "To work here?"

Westin nearly choked. "What?"

"As a listener or whatever you might call yourself? Hely agreed you'd be good at it." Sun found Hely again across the room, then cut off a snarl and turned his head away. "At least it's warm in here. You'd never have to worry about that again."

Sun could not be serious.

"I suppose I could work here." Westin put some humor into his voice so that Sun would turn back to him. "Listening, hmm? Do you think that would be enough to live on? No one would pay me for anything else."

"Fuck you." Sun's voice shook despite the venom. "You're joking about it. You're actually joking. You weren't even going to stay at the barracks and teach? You were just going to leave? You were going to come in, probably say not a single fae-blessed word about this, and never be seen again? Just like that?"

"No." Westin raised his voice. "No, I wouldn't have. And it was never 'just like that.' Do you think this is easy?"

Sun reared back then tossed his head. "Were you going to speak to me about it if I hadn't found you here? You were going to vanish, weren't you? You weren't even going to tell me."

"Sun." Westin reached across the table but Sun snatched his hand away. "Sun, I would have told you."

Sun crossed his arms. "You don't have to pretend I was on your mind. You don't need to be nice with me." He squeezed his eyes closed. "*Fuck*."

Westin raised his voice again and made it firm enough to smack sense into an angry brat. "I would have told you." Each word was clear, even if Westin's throat hurt with everything he hadn't said. "It's part of why I waited this long. I didn't want to say…"

"I suppose you'll get married next," Sun interrupted, gaze suddenly very sharp.

"*What*?" Westin wasn't used to arguing, which might have been why he was so lost. "I'm getting married?" He gestured to the air around him. "Wouldn't I have been with such a person as I worried over this? Wouldn't they be with me now?"

"Friends can share burdens too," Sun insisted stubbornly.

"What has that got to do with it?" Westin demanded in return. "Speaking with friends is enough for me." He had no idea what Sun's muttered growls were about, but he gestured around him again, to the lovers who were not there. "I've no expectations to hand-fast with anyone." That was obvious, or should have been.

Sun drew in a long breath, and as he let it out, it was as if his temper went with it. In its place was Sun smiling with teeth, leaning back to observe Westin with cool interest.

"Who is it you've got your eye on? Someone here? One of the other outguards closer to your age? Maybe you can retire together and become sworn guards to some noble who won't give two shits about how caring you are. You wouldn't be a palace guard, not you. You never even linger at the barracks, even when you need the rest."

That was true. Westin only went into the palace proper when business demanded it.

"I am going to return home." Westin knew better than to snap back at the brat when he was like this, and yet he was doing it anyway, probably shocking Hely all over again. "I am not planning on marrying," he added through gritted teeth because what would have been a calm statement of fact only a few days before was now painful to say. "I don't even have a regular lover."

Sun's eyebrows went high. His smile grew meaner "You don't? How *young* and foolish of me to think you did. It's all casual lovers then? *Friends*?" He nearly spat the word.

"What are you talking about?" Westin would have grabbed him and dragged him over the table if it would have made Sun make sense and not only crow triumphantly about prodding Westin into rash action. "If one of us at this table has a plethora of lovers, it's you, not me. Whoever gave you *those*, for example." He started to jab a finger at the ear cuffs but then realized what he was doing.

Sun's eyes were wide and shining. Vulnerable, Westin might have said. As soft as Sun's suddenly trembling lips.

"Lovers," Sun said quietly. "But not friends. Not like you, West."

Westin was breathing hard and regretted it. "I didn't mean to snarl at you." He shook his head to banish the strange, stinging jealously that he didn't like and had no right to have. "I'm sorry. I don't want to ever treat you like that."

"You don't?" Sun asked before his expression went blank and his gaze was suddenly elsewhere.

Westin wasn't used to so many feelings hitting him at once. Only Sun could do that to him, but that wasn't Sun's fault. Westin sighed and brought his voice back to his normal low register. "I want you to know more kindness than anger. I'm sure you've had enough of that."

Without looking at him, Sun still managed to glare at him. "Did I ask for that from you?"

Westin tried to pause, to consider that the brat had once been the wolfling for a reason, but, well, "Yes."

Sun turned toward him, mouth open.

Westin sought to be better but his answer remained the same. After a tup, or when lying side by side near a fire, or seated together in inns not nearly as nice as this one, Sun looked at him and asked for Westin to take care of him. "Yes, you do, lark."

Sun blinked rapidly, maybe for the name only heard in private moments. Then he was sweet, overly so, leaning forward and biting his lip prettily. "I don't want pity from you, Westin, with your gentle upbringing and your kindly ways." Scorn hit harder from someone lovely. "The one everyone asks for favors, but who never asks for anything for himself. Until tonight, it seems. All it takes is Solace House. No one else could ever manage it, could they?"

"Your bath will be ready momentarily—oh no." Hely was at their table, glancing from Westin to Sun and then back to Westin with his eyebrows raised high. "If there's going to be trouble, perhaps I ought to call an outguard."

Sun laughed at the joke, then seemed mad about it.

Westin sighed as he held up his hands. "There's no trouble." Though there might be a problem. "Sun, I was going to tell you. Please believe me."

"What does it matter if I do or don't?" Sun wondered, still trying to sound distant.

"I don't like you angry with me. I never have." Westin would get mocked forever by Hely for being so biddable for someone half his age, but that was the truth of it. "Upsetting you upsets me."

"But you'll leave just fine."

Westin would have reached for Sun's hand, but Sun didn't seem ready to offer one. He wrapped his arms around himself and scowled at the table. The posture made him seem a young noble used to being indulged who had been told no for the first time.

For all his occasional brattiness, Sun was not actually all that indulged. An outguard's life was hard and generally lonely, and the years before Sun had joined had likely been worse than Westin ever wanted to imagine. Sun's mood now might only be that Sun was not used to having close friends, and therefore not used to losing them.

Westin wanted to haul him across the table more than ever. A mad impulse that he doubted Sun would enjoy.

"No one can do this forever," he explained again, gently, to Sun and to the listening Hely. "Aging comes for us all, but it comes faster for those without much time to rest."

"And the winters scare you now," Sun said, almost miserable.

"And winter bothers me more now, yes." Westin pulled his hands to his lap to curl them into fists. "I don't think... I don't think I can do a winter on the road anymore. Not even in the south." Where the winters were more wet than cold. "And I wouldn't take assignments from anyone in the south anyway. They've earned them." He ignored how Sun muttered that *of course he wouldn't*. "You're younger," Westin tried again. "You just haven't considered all of this yet."

"You keep saying that." Sun brought his gaze up to pin Westin to his seat. "I have been left to fend for myself since I learned to walk and you think I don't know how hard life can be?"

Westin shook his head. "I never thought that, though I *am* sorry that you're so young and already have known such difficulties. But that's why I want you to know more comforts. Why I didn't want to upset you. If it...." Westin frowned at the ache in his wrist, worsened by how tightly clenched his hands were. "If it pains you to think of me gone, maybe I can stay on a few more years."

"Don't say that!" Sun glared for that too. "You think I'd ask that of you?" He sucked in a breath, then his voice fell to a trembling whisper. "*Could* I ask that of you?"

He asked it as if he had no idea what he could persuade Westin to do. Westin didn't think it wise to inform him.

"I don't like you unhappy," he reiterated, "even at your brattiest."

"That's because you're soft." Sun was quiet. "It's no surprise that you're leaving, except to me. Stupid, *young* me."

Hely made a small sound, an objection very likely.

"Sun," Westin tried.

Sun didn't let him get out more than that. "Will you tell me where you're going when you decide? That's why you came here, right? To worry over how to do it?"

"Clever boy," Hely murmured.

Westin refused to be judged for that at least. "It's not easy, leaving."

Sun shrugged. "Seems to be for most people."

Westin was not someone who growled or snapped or snarled. But his tone was sharp. "If it was easy, lark, would I need to seek peace now? Would we be fighting like this if I could just walk away?"

Hely caught his breath.

Sun stared at Westin with wide, wide eyes before abruptly turning to Hely. He lifted one hand as if to ask for something, but then curled his fingers into his palm and stood up. "My bath is ready? That's what you came to tell us? Thank you." His manners were perfect even as his gaze skittered away from Westin's. "Westin came here to find peace, so I should leave him to it. He won't get that with me around, will he?"

"That's not why," Westin began, but Hely's glance told him to tread lightly, so he switched subjects. "If you want to leave your things somewhere, my room is at the end of the hall on the second level. Use whatever soaps or oils you like. I'll pay for them."

"It's just down that way," Hely directed, guiding Sun once Sun had picked up his belongings. Sun walked off without turning back. Westin watched him disappear, then reached for the wine Sun had gotten for him and drank about half of it.

He noticed several glances sent his way and wondered with distracted alarm if he'd been loud. He didn't think so, but Sun could get Westin to do things he never ordinarily would. He imagined himself shouting at Sun and nearly rose out of his seat to go apologize. He only didn't because he wasn't entirely sure he'd raised his voice, but if he had, Sun would probably have found it funny. More proof of how Sun had Westin wrapped around his finger, to rile up or calm down as he saw fit.

That thought wasn't entirely fair. Westin had wrapped *himself* around Sun's finger. He could've stopped at any time. Traveled by different roads to be found less easily. Not given in to Sun's whining. Talked with Sun when they ran into each other but not let Sun lead him around by the cock like the aging sapwit he was.

If Sun had even done that. *Friends*, he had called them, but implied more.

Westin had the rest of the wine and noted that his hand shook as he set the empty cup down. So he closed his eyes and took a deep breath to hold and then let out. The thunder seemed to be moving away but the rain continued to pound onto the roof. There'd be no travel for anyone who could avoid it tonight. Solace House would get no more customers unless someone was very determined.

A customer at a table somewhere behind him had been served dinner, offering tantalizing hints of gravy and a roast and a heady, lush dark wine. Sun was in a bath room, in a tub of hot water, debating which soaps or scents to wash himself with. He might choose something floral; he'd noticed the roses and violets enough to differentiate between the two.

He had fine tastes that ought to be indulged more, by someone who understood that Sun at his most charming was Sun trying to get people to like him so they would want to keep him around, or maybe so he could control them and feel safe. As long as that was understood, all would be well. A charming Sun was a Sun hiding, and was so far from the Sun who snapped for Westin to stay in bed and drink his broth like a sick man ought to that he might as well have been a different person.

Or, a side of the same person, but one Westin was glad to never deal with. He wasn't sure what he would have done if he had first met the smiling, flirtatious Sunlark of South Burrow. Probably flushed and gone as witless as everyone else.

He'd done that anyway, hadn't he? And for the side of Sun who barked at him and demanded Westin's cock as if it belonged to him. That said something. Westin had no idea what, but something.

Friends. That's what it said. Sun considered Westin enough of a friend to be rude, even when feeling lusty, and Westin had wounded him greatly by not telling him sooner that he planned to leave. The shortening days *had* been on Westin's mind during their last encounter, but Sun had been in such a lively mood, and Westin had known that would be their only visit until their quick meetup at the barracks before winter weather would keep them apart, so he had let Sun fill the silence with stories of his adventures over the past weeks and said not a word of his plans. When Westin had allowed himself to acknowledge the ache in his chest, it had only been to remind himself to savor the time left and to ensure Sun was happy.

That felt like cowardice now.

He should have at least told Sun how much he would miss him. Westin *already* counted the days they were apart and started looking around for Sun to appear if the weeks turned to months. Leaving the Outguard meant Westin would lose that even if he could convince Sun to come visit him.

Which... he likely couldn't, now. That was what hesitation had cost him. Or maybe that always would have been the outcome. It was Westin's family's habit not to reach for things, to be content with what they had. If Sun had a family habit or motto, it was undoubtedly more along the lines of rely on only yourself, or don't trust easily, and Westin had failed him there.

Even that day at the river and the night at the inn that followed, Westin hadn't said a word. He had let Sun head out in the morning, only mentioning something about their meeting in the capital, and Sun had huffed and muttered against Westin's chest before setting off, walking alongside his horse because he had insisted on taking Westin's cock twice and Westin had no sense where Sun was concerned.

Sun knew better than to ride cock in the dark of their room and then demand it again at sunrise. Yet he'd done it anyway. Reckless.

Westin felt himself frowning.

But Sun *wasn't* reckless, except for those fights in his younger days. Sun was a clever, calculating, thorough outguard who, as he often pointedly said, was smart enough to be selfish when it came to taking care of himself.

Sun did what he wanted. The Outguard was a means for a better life for him, and he reveled in the work. But he was not reckless. In fact, if Westin had been the one to do something like that while knowing it would leave him too sore to comfortably ride a horse, Sun would have chastised him for it, and probably more harshly than Hely with a far too flirtatious new worker.

A presence at his elbow made Westin clear his frown. Then he raised his head to meet Hely's questioning stare.

Part Two

"I HAVE SOME TIME if you'd like to sit in a booth for a while." Hely wasn't really asking. He knew Westin well enough to know phrasing it as a question would end with more polite insistence that he was fine, even though Westin was decidedly not fine. He was ruffled and guilty and worried that the hurt, furious brat taking a bath might never want to talk to him again.

"Apparently," Hely continued smoothly, "he ordered tea for you. Not a pot, just a cup. With milk in it that he wanted warmed first so that your drink would stay hot longer." Hely reached behind him to take the cup that Alit was bringing over. He nodded to Alit, waited for Westin to accept the inevitable and stand up, then handed the cup to him.

The tea was so hot the cup warmed his hands. The steam smelled of citrus oils and sharp leaves, the bitterness tempered only slightly by the milk. Not a hugely popular blend, but Westin had odd tastes.

Alit was staring at him and looking startled when Westin opened his eyes from inhaling the steam, but she quickly turned and hurried back to the kitchens.

Westin had a sip of his gifted tea, and then another, inwardly reveling in the gift from Sun as much as he delighted in the taste.

Hely's glance said Hely could see all of that, but he didn't say a word. He simply began to weave around tables in the direction of one of the open booths. Westin followed him, pausing to grab the bag he'd stashed beneath his table. He carried it in one hand and considered what angle Hely might use and what he ought to say in response, although Hely had years of experience at conversation, and anyway, Westin was sure that his feelings were already visible to Hely and anyone else who knew him well.

Not the brat, or so he hoped with a drink in his hand that said the brat might not know *now*, but he could guess. And soon.

Westin exhaled heavily and didn't wait to drop onto one of the cushioned benches that made up the booth. The booth itself was shaped nearly like a horseshoe, with wooden benches backed by walls that reached the ceiling. The far wall at the other end of the booth had a window with curtains that could be drawn for privacy. Opposite that, instead of a wall was a curtain that reached the floor, made of a red fabric that didn't block all sound or all light, but blocked enough of it to make the space feel secluded. The common room of Solace House was never all that loud anyway. Conversations, wherever they took place, were meant to be private.

The booths were simply *more* private, and quieter, for those who needed that without the implications of one of the rooms. Although the built-in cabinets below the bench seats held all kinds of supplies, from books on philosophy and poetry, to candles, to towels, to more oils, some of the perfumed variety meant to diffuse through the room to aid in finding calm, and some for an entirely different purpose.

Hely peered beyond the curtain over the window at the storm, clucked his tongue, and went about lighting a few candles and placing them in the holders on the top of the shortest section of bench, the one beneath the window. Then he drew the large curtain closed behind him and sat opposite Westin on the other cushioned bench. There was a small space between them. Enough for their knees not to touch and then some, but not enough to dance or move freely or have more than a handful of people in the booth at one time.

Westin, feeling stubborn, had another drink of his lovely tea, then got up enough to put the cup next to one of the candles. Without much to focus on except the candle smoke and the more distant murmurs from the common room, he began to tap his fingers on his knee. Which Hely would note, so Westin pulled in a breath and then reached into his bag to pull out a skein of leafy-green yarn and his knitting needles. He counted along a row to be sure of his place and arranged the finished portion of the scarf across his lap. Then he stopped.

"Take your time."

"Did you need a break?" Westin asked immediately. "I wasn't going to ask for conversation. If you're after a moment of rest, we can just sit."

Hely's lips quirked. "You aren't even trying to avoid talking. You will genuinely sit there, unhappy and worrying, to give me a moment of rest. That said, because you have such a disciplined mind and such a steady nature, if you'd truly wanted peace tonight, you would have found it, no matter who walked through the door."

Westin thought that description made him sound about as exciting as a rock. Which was in itself a strange thought to have. Westin didn't want to be exciting. But he might have at least wanted to be *interesting*. It might have made him feel less tired, ancient, hobbled, and stupid. He liked being steady and reliable, but it wasn't much of a draw, was it? And he'd wanted a draw. He could admit that now.

He really was a fool.

"I didn't think of what my leaving would be like for him," he admitted aloud because he deserved some shame. "I didn't want to. I knew it would upset him, but I mostly thought that it would be like any other outguard retiring. Maybe he'd feel it a little more, I hoped, although then I also knew—believed—I was flattering myself to think that. And I didn't want to say goodbye. Even if I could convince him to visit me once in a while, it wouldn't be the same."

"Will you still visit us here?" Hely asked unhappily. "Or is this the last time we will all see you?"

Westin dropped his head to accept the reproach. "You'll see me. You know I don't live far from here. Well, they don't—*I* won't, soon. I've been avoiding thinking about afterward and what it will be like. I wasn't deliberately hiding this from everyone. But they were right: Chaus, Sun, anyone else who guessed. I can't take another winter with the cold, and the dark, and the time away from—everyone. It gets worse every year, but I thought I could bear it a little longer. If I didn't talk about it, it was because it sounds ridiculous, giving in to some frost."

Hely seemed about to say something so Westin gently shook his head. "It's not ridiculous, perhaps, but it *feels* that way. Mornings after a night on the ground are harder now, even without snow or ice. And he's...."

He didn't finish but Hely nodded. "I understand."

But he didn't move, waiting for Westin to keep going. It always took a while; Westin wasn't used to laying out his feelings and strange worries. He had to be poked and prodded, and... apparently Hely wasn't the only one to have seen that about him.

"Ah," Westin sighed it. "I'll explain that to him, if he lets me." The possibility that Sun wouldn't allow him anything anymore and simply move on was very real. Westin rubbed his temple. "I should have at least mentioned the idea to him, even if it did show my years and exhaustion. It's not like Sun doesn't already know my age. He wouldn't have been surprised. At me leaving, yes. But not at why. He's not even really surprised about that now."

"No, that's not what upset him."

Despite Hely's agreement, Westin remained unsatisfied. "I understand that he's angry," he said carefully. "But he shouldn't be this upset. I was going to tell him. He should at least trust that. I was going to tell everyone."

Hely waited a moment. "Is that really why you believe he's upset?"

The moment he took was as pointed as the question that followed it, so Westin paused as well to reconsider Sun's words.

Sun had said that was why, or at least, he'd spoken harshly when he'd asked if Westin hadn't been going to tell him. If that wasn't what he'd meant, then Sun had been pretending with him. Westin tensed. If Sun had been pretending, then Sun had been protecting himself. From *Westin*.

Westin went cold. "I didn't know I mattered that much to him." Enough for Sun to lie and hide. Enough to feel betrayed, when Westin had only ever wanted Sun to feel safe.

Hely was gentler than he could have been. "Tell me, when your family dropped the fifth beat from their name, did they also change the family motto to 'keep your head down and reach for nothing?'"

Westin glanced toward the curtain out of reflex more than any real fear. *Corilyeth* meant pitying looks or sneers from other nobles, and stiffness or discomfort from most outguards. Some knew, usually those who had joined around the same time Westin had, but Westin wasn't the only one in the Outguard to use a strange name. He doubted there even was a place called South Burrow, for one. He left people with their secrets unexamined and usually got the same courtesy in return.

"Oh no. You didn't tell him that either, did you?" Hely clearly despaired of him.

"I would have when I invited him to come visit me. If he actually came." Westin ignored the fact that he had wanted Sun to meet his family for years now. Not for any particular reason, he'd told himself. Only that Sun might enjoy rest in a place that cost him nothing, and hopefully wouldn't find the small estate too boring. Yet the truth beneath all of that was that Westin had wanted Sun to stay. He'd wanted Sun to be content with a boring life with a boring man. It was almost shameful, which was likely why Westin hadn't wanted to face it.

Nonetheless, it had taken Hely only moments of observing Westin around Sun to suss that out. Which meant it was only luck that Sun had not.

Westin pushed away that possibility for the present and considered the friend patiently waiting for him to own up to what an ass he was.

"I would have missed you, Hely." Westin said to make it as plain as he could. "I will visit. You and your husband could even visit me. I'll be happy to have you."

"You will be, more than likely because you will be a little bored." The candlelight made Hely seem briefly wicked, as he might have been when much younger or when not working. "Before tonight, I would have said a completely quiet life would suit you, but now I'd say the perfect amount of danger and worry excites you. Well, perhaps not *excites*, but keeps you sharp. That is probably another reason you stayed in the Outguard so long. It wasn't only him; it was having something to do, problems to solve. Although," Hely was wicked again, "you like doing him as well."

Westin sighed loudly in exasperation.

Hely was undeterred. "Yet he doesn't know about you, your family, your home." He clucked his tongue. "Westin."

"I used to imagine bringing him home to meet everyone. I should have recognized that dream for what it was, not that it matters now. He's hurt." Westin shut his eyes. "I hurt him." And Sun had let Westin see it before he'd tucked it away and swanned off to enjoy some comfort at Westin's expense. Westin hoped he spent a small fortune in there. Because Sun deserved it, and because it meant Sun was showing Westin that he was angry—hurt.

"He cares enough to show it," Westin realized aloud. "He thinks he's losing a friend." A close friend. Perhaps even a best friend.

Hely raised his voice ever so slightly. "He thinks he's losing *you*. You are, if you don't mind me saying so, an *exceptional* friend to have, Westin. And I'm not even a regular lover to enjoy the rest of you as well."

Westin went still, inhaling candle smoke and fading perfume from whoever had used the booth last. He had only just put it in those terms to himself, but of course Hely had already seen it.

"I've never had a regular lover," Westin confessed, barely above a murmur. "Never thought I did, anyway."

"Because you never asked for one?" Hely had that despairing tone again. "Westin. You're not your family name. You're more than that. The land wouldn't fail because you wanted to take something for your own, especially not a companion to love you. Isn't your sister married? Don't your brothers flirt with anyone and everyone at the markets?"

"It's different," Westin argued stiffly. Responsibility mattered. Sense and duty mattered. Westin was not exceptional and that was what people liked about him. He was steady, and somewhat boring, and only likely to get more so over time. That was what made him so suitable for his role. No one was going to reach for him and he certainly was never going to *take*.

Unless pushed to, repeatedly. Then he would grow hot and start to snap back before finally reaching for what had been so consistently offered.

Westin swallowed dryly but left the tea where it was.

Regular lover implied deeper friendship, deeper connection. Implied frequency. Implied that Westin should have discussed his worries with the person who was closer to him than anyone else before he'd made the decision.

It did not imply what Westin wished it did.

"I'm reliable," he answered after a revealing silence. "And a friend. And safe for him to be himself around." *Soft*, Sun had said, with something fond in it. "A soft-touch," Westin corrected himself out loud, "who gives in to his ridiculous requests even when I know they're ridiculous."

"You're generous," Hely countered with a little smile. "Those are your qualities—as you think he sees them. I might disagree there, but even if what you imagine *were* true and those were the only good traits you possess, those aren't small things. They would be especially important qualities for someone who likely grew up without anyone like that in his life. He charmed Min at the bar. He might have charmed me if I hadn't seen him with you."

"He snarls at me." Westin was resigned to it.

Hely shook his head. "He *trusts you* to snarl at you. And you, as might be expected by anyone who knows you even slightly, *are* safe, *are* giving, *are* reliable. Until tonight, I'd bet that you passed his every test. Enough that when you hurt him just now, he was so genuinely surprised that it showed."

Westin realized he was gripping the needles too tightly.

"I was also hurt," Hely reminded him.

"I said I was sorry." Westin paused, then tossed his head. "Well, I'm saying it now. I *am* sorry. But I *was* going to tell you tonight. And I was going to tell him... but I should have discussed it with him when I first began to consider it. I shouldn't have been embarrassed."

Hely granted him a warm smile. "Westin, you are, at least in part, what nobles ought to be. You are also, and I speak from experience, the sort to make an excellent husband."

Westin let a needle slip from his hand and had to fumble for it. "Husband?" His thoughts crashed together. "That's...." He'd never dreamed of anything that far, and if he hadn't, he doubted Sun had. "Sun is a survivor, and he's young. I don't think his greater future has even crossed his mind. He's certainly never spoken of it."

Hely was unruffled by that argument. "Maybe he doesn't know what futures are available to him."

"I didn't know Solace House also offered matchmaking services," Westin joked hoarsely, or tried to joke, although he was probably giving Hely ideas. He took a deep breath, which did not a thing to calm him. "The younger ones, the ones who join the Outguard because they have no family or few options, like Sun. They don't think they *have* futures. But they eventually realize they are welcome to stay in the barracks to teach or to count supplies—tasks will be found for them, if they've nowhere else to go. Or they discover love or a different calling on the road. *Those* are the sort of futures they might think of."

"Love on the road." Hely made the words sound different. "I see. So you have been waiting for him to do that. What if he has?"

"What?" Sun and Hely had not been alone that long. They couldn't have grown close enough to discuss something like that, no matter how good Hely was at cultivating intimacy. "He didn't mention that. He would tell me if he'd met someone. I'd hear all about it."

"Except that jewelry surprised you," Hely pointed out. "He has no family and not much money. So where did those cuffs come from?"

Westin had fallen from a roof once, thankfully onto soft ground. Even in pain with the wind knocked out of him, he'd felt better than he did after Hely hit him with that.

He had the passing, annoyed thought that Sun had no call to be angry with him for keeping secrets if Sun had been hiding lovers. But it was the sort of warm annoyance he often felt where Sun was concerned. It was followed by longing, bitter and sweet, and then acceptance of the truth, no matter how much he'd grieve later.

"He deserves to be happy," Westin said, and meant it. "And spoiled or indulged more." If Sun had learned to show others his vulnerable side, that could only be good for him. "If he's found someone, or several someones, to keep him happy, then I'm glad. Or if he's looking for that, then... then good."

"What if he looks here tonight? That won't bother you?"

Everyone kept insisting Westin was generous. He didn't see why Hely would think him lying now. Westin was not territorial. "Why should it?"

Hely shocked him with a smug grin. "Westin, darling, you are spitting out sparks like a log on a fire. You very much *are* bothered."

"What?" Westin was doing no such thing. He was knitting, or, he was going to. He was breathing deeply and he wasn't calm but he ought to at least *appear* calm. Very few people would have thought otherwise. One was across from him and the other was probably looking for someone to charm right at that moment.

"*Sparks.*" Hely was enjoying himself. "Your boy is a gift."

"He's not..."

"How long has it been since you two last touched each other?" Hely pressed, more thoughtful than gleeful.

"About two months." Westin was too surprised to lie, not that he would have; Hely would have seen through it.

"So little?" Hely clucked his tongue and ignored or failed to notice Westin's displeasure at that. "What I mean by that is that it has only been a few weeks since you saw him last, and yet you looked at him as though you wanted to haul him to you and have him on the table in front of everyone."

Westin didn't fumble the needle a second time, but only because he held it painfully tight. "When I first saw him?"

"Pretty much the entire time." Hely was merciless. "Yet no welcome hug or kiss, not even a clasp of hands. From either of you. I was both confused and intrigued."

Westin shook his head. "Sun doesn't want..."

Hely shut him up neatly. "Your brat would have been happy to have been taken on that table. By *you*. He flattered me, and Min, and the bath attendant. He *hungers* for you. Your attention. Your care. Your cock too, I'm sure. Do you truly not see that?"

Westin burned like a flustered youth. "No one hungers for me."

"Hmm," Hely said, then nothing else for several long moments, a cue for Westin to think over what had been discussed. When Hely did talk again, it was only to add, "You haven't been knitting."

Westin began to knit out of reflex, hands quick, thoughts quicker and far less orderly. Outguards spent a great deal of time alone and all had ways to pass the time, like whittling, or reading, or working with fibers like this. Westin mostly made scarves, which were easy, and outguards always needed more warm clothes for rough travels. Westin worried as well, and maybe many of them knew that and were happy to accept his gifts to appease his anxiety. Sun knew it, even if he hadn't been wearing the last scarf Westin had made for him. Those cuffs, but no scarf.

"Have you been hiding this from me all this time?" Hely wondered, not giving Westin much of a chance to answer. "Not him," he explained before Westin got out more than a quiet objection. "You weren't hiding your Sun from me; you were keeping your secret dreams about him to yourself. But *this*." He gestured toward Westin's furiously clacking knitting needles. "I never expected you to be the sort to claim territory, but you shouldn't be ashamed of it."

"I have *not* claimed territory." That, Westin had never done. Even the family land was for the family and those working on it. It wasn't *his*.

Hely ignored that. "You think he will charm himself into a bed tonight. To sweet-talk that jewelry from someone, he must have been quite charming indeed."

Westin couldn't summon any anger over that, which was more proof that he wasn't territorial. "Yes. He is very charming when he wants to be. Not with me, but he doesn't need to with me." Westin, the soft-touch. "I've always liked that. He can be himself with me. He doesn't have to put out so much effort."

Hely leaned forward. "He tracked you down here. I would say he thinks you're worth some effort. He probably thinks that even now despite how you stabbed him with the idea of losing you. What surprises me, aside from witnessing this side of you, is that he *had* to track you down. Why don't you travel together? The Outguard allows that, doesn't it?"

About to insist that he didn't need someone else with him who had their own assignments to worry about, Westin abruptly stopped.

"He did say something about that once," he finally admitted, flushing hot with embarrassment, "in his insolent way." Sun had found Westin sick in the spare room of a public house in a little village. He had been ranting at Westin at the time. Westin had agreed that he'd deserved to be ranted at; he should have done better. But summer and spring illnesses happened too. Sickness wasn't only a winter problem. And though Westin had been exhausted when he'd first ridden into that village, and exhaustion made bodies weaker, that didn't mean he could control catching the sniffles... or something stronger than mere sniffles.

Sun had been furious. Worried, now that Westin knew for sure what that looked like on the brat. Worried enough to let it show.

Fuck, Westin had messed up.

"Hely, if I set it up, could I cover the costs of his visits here if he wants to come back?"

Hely's eyes widened. Then he smiled, fond but exasperated. "Wouldn't it be easier to tell him that you want to care for him? He might need to hear that. He might not have ever heard it before."

A new hurt in an evening of them, but then, Westin hadn't really come to Solace House for peace. He'd come to settle himself, and that required the truth. That was always a little troubling, but also always worth it in the end.

"He might get difficult." The brat was a brat and would stay a brat if Westin had anything to say about it. "I'll have to phrase it right. Telling Sun what to do only works while fucking, and even then, he can be stubborn." Defiance and obedience at the same time, beautiful and not even remotely peaceful. And yet Westin ached for him.

"He seems to have no problem with other people giving him things." Hely wasn't even saying it to be mean; the observation was gentle. "Why would he object if you wish to?"

"Because I'm not his lover," Westin explained, some tartness in his voice until he heard himself and remembered the look on Sun's face when Westin had said nearly the same thing to him. "I *am* his lover," he corrected. "A regular lover. But only one of them, and as friends without any romance."

Hely smiled and Westin was surprised at how much he resented it.

"Westin, you are my friend, so I will be kind now, kinder than I could be. You should *ask* your brat why he came here tonight. Or why he lets you call him brat, for that matter." Hely lifted a hand. "Don't tell me he's not your brat. He wasn't going to spend money here. He didn't come to Solace House with anything on his mind but you, although he had heard of us. And why do most people come to Solace House?"

"For solace." Which meant peace for some, comfort for others. Often quiet or calm, but not always. The critical requirement was to feel at ease, and for that, people needed to trust. They had to feel safe. For some, Solace House was one of the few places where they might do so, which was why they gladly paid higher prices.

And Sun had come here for him.

"And he came here for you." Hely echoed Westin's thoughts as though he could read them on Westin's stunned face. He continued to smile but now with satisfaction. He sat back and said nothing else while Westin stared blankly at the curtain to the common room and grew so hot he could feel it in the toes he no longer had.

After a few moments, Westin began to knit again, slower.

"I don't believe it," he finally murmured, although Hely probably knew that already. "Even if I admit that my future will be dull without him, it would be dull with him. *For* him, surely. That is to say, he wouldn't be a captive. He could leave. I can't make him do anything. I don't want to, but I just never could. Except for...." The needles went still. "He's furious with me and you think I should try to convince him to marry me?"

"I didn't say that," Hely remarked, *beyond* satisfied. "*You* did. *I* merely pointed out that you would make a good husband."

"Dull," Westin insisted.

"Does he seem like someone who would allow things to get too boring?" Hely's amusement was audible, then drowned out by a rising murmur from beyond the curtain.

Westin turned toward the trouble, absently reaching for the weapon he wasn't currently carrying. It wasn't much of a commotion, but raised voices in Solace House were so unusual that he had tensed before he recognized the sounds of Sun being stubborn and rude.

"*Where are they*?" Sun demanded, not shouting, but loud for the Solace common room.

"Not so charming now," Hely remarked.

"Are they in there?" Sun asked again, leaving Westin to wonder which worker had darted a look to or gestured at the booth he shared with Hely. He didn't blame whoever it was; Sun was every inch an intimidating outguard when he chose to be.

Then the curtain was torn open, and Westin accepted that a worker might have been flustered by Sun for entirely different reason.

Sun stood in the booth's entrance with no pants and no shoes. His hair was damp and slightly curled from the heat of the bath. His bared skin looked warm to the touch, the trail of hair from his chest to his stomach dark with water because he apparently hadn't bothered to fully dry himself. His breeches clung to his wet legs as well, as though he'd flung himself from the bath, barely attempted to dress enough for decency, and then stormed into the common room in search of them.

In search of *him*. Westin's eyes were stinging, dry because he was staring, struggling to look away from all of the damp, hot skin being displayed for anyone who cared to look.

And plenty did.

Alit was blushing fiercely in the distance, visible over Sun's shoulder, although Westin was more interested in the shoulder itself, and then Sun's chest again, before he belatedly remembered that Hely was watching him pant over Sun and brought his gaze up.

Sun was frowning, glancing from Hely to Westin with a brief, deeper frown at the unfinished scarf in Westin's lap.

"Honestly." Hely stood up, shooing away the oglers and shutting the curtain again behind Sun so briskly that Sun jumped. "You may as well come all the way in."

"Does that cost extra?" Sun returned, but with distracted interest and not attitude. Then he seemed to correct himself, bowing his head to Hely. "Sorry, I..."

"You're not sorry." Hely sat back down and gestured for Sun to do the same, but Sun seemed stuck where he was. He frowned down at the knitting as if absolutely confused, so Westin began to use his needles again although he wasn't counting a single stitch. He could take the mess apart later.

Sun finally turned that frown on Hely, his contrition short-lived. "What, he's not good enough for you?"

Westin didn't get a chance to comment. Hely beamed a smile which Sun riled up further, though he turned that wrath on Westin.

"Are you spending the money you would have spent on a tumble on me and my bath?" He jabbed an accusing finger at Westin. "That is *enough*. You can't take care of yourself even when it comes fucking or...or... talking or whatever they call it here? You grew up adored and cared for; I can tell because you refuse to be selfish. Selfish is useful! If you were selfish, maybe you'd...."

"What?" Westin prompted, mesmerized by the impatient, embarrassed, half-naked brat who hadn't even taken the time to dry off before he'd sought Westin out. "Maybe I'd what?"

"Yes, go on." Hely was nothing but encouraging.

Sun raked his gaze over Westin as if looking one last time for some sign of a passionate encounter, then turned forcefully to Hely.

"Did he tell you about how sick he got last year?" Sun gave Westin's general direction another accusing jab. "I bet he didn't, and not only because he barely remembers most of it." Westin stopped knitting and straightened, although of course they both ignored him. "I found him, and I had to walk the delirious idiot back to the nearest village because I couldn't get him on his horse. I'd only even found him off the road because I had a feeling he'd collapsed somewhere. They'd told me all about him when I'd reached the village in the first place. When I was..."

"Looking for him?" Hely guessed.

Sun nodded without pausing. "They told me that they thought the last outguard had shown signs of the fever many of them were sick with, but they hadn't been able to convince him to stay. 'People are expecting me,' he'd told them." He rounded on Westin. "It could have waited."

"Not for that much longer," Westin argued, although since it had ended up waiting anyway with him too weak to continue on, it was a fool's argument. But since he was already a fool, he didn't care as much when he heard himself asking with obvious surprise, "You were there looking for me?"

Sun stared at him, his lips parted.

"What else?" Hely was having a good time. "How else does he need to be selfish, Sun? He might need to hear it and I don't mind listening."

Sun tore his gaze from Westin, looked at Hely, and then closed his eyes long enough to say, "The frostbite." When Sun looked at Westin again, he was bubbling up with fury. *Worry,* Westin knew now. *Fear.*

Sun took a breath and focused on Hely. "That was when I was still new to being out on the road on my own and we barely knew each other, but everyone heard about it. Years later, I find out that it was because he gave away his blanket and bedroll!" He gestured his outrage while Hely nodded understandingly and gave Westin a displeased look. "'Someone needed it more,' he said. Everyone in the barracks scolded him or rolled their eyes and not one of them offered to go with him to ensure he didn't do it again! Not one!"

"The blanket wouldn't have made that much of a difference, Sun," Westin explained, not for the first time, "not in that storm."

"You shut up." Sun was back to glaring at Westin. "I asked why he didn't have someone to go with him as some outguards do. They said he never asked for one. I couldn't get over it. I still can't."

"*You* travel alone." Westin had to point it out because Sun was smaller and had a temper, something Westin worried over.

Sun huffed. "I can take care of myself. I'm not soft like you."

"He is, isn't he?" Hely reached out to encircle Sun's wrist. Sun let him, seeming confused but not angered by the gentle touch. "You noticed that early on, I bet. It's a remarkable quality for someone who has been an outguard for as long as he has."

"Remarkable," Sun echoed quietly. Then shook himself and began glaring again. "He shouldn't even be an outguard!" It was said with finality, and not even Westin's wounded gasp slowed Sun down. "He's so good when he's asked to make decisions. He's *incredible* at resolving disputes, which isn't officially our job but it does make things easier. He's so good at it that a lot of the others think he ought to be in charge. But he doesn't like a fight. He *will* fight—and he will end those fights." Sun gave Westin a hot look. "But he doesn't like it. And he doesn't like seeing some of the things we see."

Hely made a disapproving noise. "Do you?"

"No, he doesn't," Westin answered for Sun before Sun could dismiss the question. "He has a kind heart despite how he likes to act."

He expected more outrage, a hotter glare. Instead, Sun dropped his shoulders. "You see? I don't even know why he joined."

"I wasn't really needed at home for a while," Westin said truthfully. "And I wanted to see more places, and it was decent money." He ignored Sun's scoff. "I could have left earlier, I suppose. But others were expecting me to keep going."

"Too. Nice." Sun growled both words then appealed to Hely again. "The sickness was the same. He had fever dreams... nightmares. He was in that village for a fortnight to recover, and he kept trying to leave earlier out of some stupid idea about *duty*. As if he's a noble or something. He's smarter than that."

Hely gently held Sun's wrist again, then released him. "Were you with him the whole time?"

Sun's eyes went wide. With no shirt, the faint color rising in his cheeks would be visible as it spread down his chest. Well, if they'd had more candlelight, it would have been. He glanced to Westin. "There was no one else. I'm no healer but I can fetch water and clean messes."

"*Sun.*" Westin sighed the name.

"I stayed," Sun told Hely, glancing to Westin again. "I could do that. I even offered...."

"To continue on with him." Hely didn't need to guess since Westin had told him. "And he smiled and insisted he was fine on his own?"

"I *was* fine!" Westin defended himself but hurried to calm Sun. "Not that I didn't want your company, lark. But you had other things to do and didn't need to be polite to an...." He trailed to silence at the flare of hurt Sun didn't hide in time. "The offer was made in earnest. I apologize. But it really wasn't necessary to burden yourself."

"Oh, I see." Sun crossed his arms. "You can pay for me to have the nicest bath of my life—"

"Surprised you left it so early," Hely cut in.

"I couldn't trust you with him." Sun stopped short, then narrowed his eyes at Hely, who stared back, a subtly pleased matchmaker. A moment later, Sun let his arms fall. His expression was all silky displeasure and it was aimed at Westin. "If you can pay for that, and for tea, and offer your room, I can offer to ride with you to make sure you *stay alive*. Unless you think I'm not capable?"

A challenge.

Westin's palms itched with the urge to haul the cocky brat into his lap, which was when he remembered he was holding knitting needles and put them aside.

"Of course you're capable. You've been an outguard since you were eighteen." Still too young for it, in Westin's opinion. Especially to be out there alone, even in times of peace as they were fortunate enough to live in now, bless the current queen. "I would never doubt you."

Hely reached out again as if to stop Sun before Sun could release some of the steam clearly about to burst from him. His tone was measured and professional. "Then why is he not allowed to care for you, Westin? Is it hard to believe that he'd want to?"

Sun immediately stopped, explosion forgotten, a puzzled line between his eyes. "Why would that be hard to believe when I've followed after him for years now?"

He met Westin's stare and whatever it held, then snapped his mouth shut.

Hely rose to his feet, not asking for room but smiling faintly when a distracted Sun moved to make way. Hely gave Westin one last look of warning, then leaned in to whisper something into Sun's ear, lips almost brushing the fae-cursed cuffs.

"*Words first*," Westin thought he heard among whatever else Hely told Sun, and then Hely slipped out from the curtain and tugged it back into place so that not even a sliver of light showed from anywhere except along the top.

"Why did you rush through your bath?" Westin wondered immediately, not demanding because he didn't make demands. He *asked*, though in this case, with an edge. "Are you cold like that? Were none of your shirts clean enough?"

The last question had an edge to it and Sun clearly heard it, because he dropped back into his slouching, sulky posture and gave Westin a defiant look.

"Maybe I'm trying to get a new ear cuff."

Westin inhaled deeply, finding traces of citrus and something herbal. It wasn't soothing. He didn't really want it to be.

"Then I'd wonder why you'd waste time in here with me. The best I offered was a bath."

Sun lifted his chin, about to snap back, but then glanced away to study the candles as if the candles were all that interesting. He shrugged. "It was a pretty good bath."

Westin didn't laugh but he did make a rough, half-stifled sound that brought Sun's attention back to him.

It was strange how little Westin felt like apologizing. "Unless you've been fucking a *very* wealthy beat-of-four, that's the nicest bath you've like to have had in years, maybe ever."

Sun smiled, mean and pleased. "Are you asking?" When Westin stared at him, momentarily lost, Sun rolled his wrist in an exaggerated manner. "Are you asking if I'm fucking a very wealthy beat-of-four?"

"You aren't." Westin wondered what Hely would make of his tone. "None of those cuffs are gold."

Sun's eyebrows went up. "You think I could get gold?"

"I think you could get gold." Westin was confident of that if nothing else. "And more than a cuff. Maybe *you* should work here."

Sun blinked several times before humming thoughtfully. "Would that mean I'd still see you?"

"Ah." The fight, such as it was, left Westin. He met Sun's challenging stare and wondered absently just when he'd begun to realize that with Sun *challenging* meant *vulnerable*. Later than he should have. But then he recognized that he must have known years ago, because he had begun responding to Sun's demands and impertinence with patient indulgence. He had just never pushed the matter. He should have. "I wasn't going to leave you." The truth said at last, and he would make Sun recognize it even if Sun never wanted to see him again. "I'm leaving the Outguard." The words still pulled at his heart, but Sun was what mattered now. "I didn't want to leave you. But... I didn't think you'd be this upset."

Sun's chin went up higher. His smile grew brighter. "Who's upset?"

Westin's palms itched again.

"These booths are for when people need moments to be themselves. To be true, whether that's their own doing, or paying someone to strip all their pretenses from them. They're to allow people to lower their shoulders without judgment. And for fucking," Westin added before Sun could be smart. "Sometimes they are for that too, or a combination of all of those things. Though most of *that* would be best done in a room."

Sun was smart with him anyway. "Yes. I did figure that out, West. I'm so terribly *young* according to you, but I'm not actually a child."

Westin shoved the knitting to the side and stood. Sun's eyes went wide and his head came up. He wet his lips.

Westin wasn't a giant, patient or otherwise, but whatever he was, Sun liked it.

"Stop that," Westin ordered, then caught his breath, surprised yet again by what Sun could get him to do and by how little he minded.

"Stop what?" Sun returned without innocence. "Not that I take orders from you."

"Except that you do." Westin breathed it, slightly shocked at hearing the words said and at him being the one to say them. "Because I care for you, and you know that, because you use it." Sun's lips slipped apart, stunned and soft. Westin refused to be distracted and repeated himself so Sun couldn't deny this. "You trust me enough to do what I say because I care for you."

He didn't know how he meant that, but every interpretation would be true, which was why he didn't elaborate.

A shiver went through Sun. He closed his mouth but apparently just to be stubborn and raise his chin for a moment. "You can't make me do anything."

Westin nodded. He couldn't. But Sun often chose to do what Westin asked of him—very often, now that Westin was allowing himself to think on it.

"That's the part that still amazes me. I can't make you, but you choose to. The fae know what Hely is going to charge me for that realization."

Sun started to frown at the mention of Hely and that was amazing too. Unless Hely had done something to offend him, the only explanation was that Sun was a hotly jealous creature, over *Westin*. Even if that was over having Westin's attention solely on him like the brat he was, it was madness. But, fae help him, Westin's heart was beating faster.

"You didn't even stop to put on a shirt before you came crashing in here." He ran his palms down Sun's sides before settling his hands heavily at Sun's waist, with Sun breathing harder and letting him.

"I don't understand." Sun tried to peer down at Westin's hands on him, but kept looking back up and jolting every time he found Westin watching him. "Wait, you and Hely were talking about me?" He pressed his lips together, then parted them for one bemused question. "Why?"

Westin wanted to press a kiss to that mouth. He resisted. Words first. Sun needed to hear them.

"Because I hurt you and I wanted to fix it," he admitted honestly. "And I was upset at the idea of possibly never seeing you again." Sun's shocked breath gave him strength for what was much tougher to say, even for an older, experienced guard. "And because I am wrapped around your finger, which Hely saw immediately. As many do, I imagine."

Instead of a preening smirk, he got a wild, uncertain stare and then Sun quickly shaking his head. "You're leaving. You were going to even before I made a scene."

"The Outguard. Not you." Westin dared to reach yet again by cupping Sun's cheek. Only for a moment, but Sun allowed that too. How long had that been something Westin might do out of bed and he hadn't noticed? Sun granted him much, and even if he didn't wear Westin's scarf, Westin had this. "I won't leave you unless you tell me to."

He wasn't expecting Sun to frown fretfully. "Don't." He broke Westin's heart and then pressed the pieces together again in almost the same breath. "Don't do that. Don't stay where you'll be miserable just to make me feel better. That still isn't being selfish. I want you to be selfish."

"Ah." Another sigh, another realization. Westin hauled a surprised Sun against him from toe to chest. Two months wasn't a small amount of time no matter what Hely thought. Westin bent his head and breathed in with his mouth against Sun's wet hair. "Oranges and rosemary? I thought you'd choose flowers."

"You don't like flowers." Sun was warm against him yet shivering faintly, probably the effects of not completely drying the water from his hair. "Not like that."

Westin nearly asked why Sun would bother trying to please him, but suspected it would only get Sun's back up. "I'd rather you wear what you like. You'll need another bath tomorrow then."

"Wes." Sun shuddered as the rare, more private version of Westin's name left him. "I'm not going to take all of your money."

"What happened to 'be selfish?'" Westin genuinely didn't understand but was also a little too dizzy to think clearly. "I can afford it."

Which was a strong reminder that he had more to tell Sun, but stroking Sun's back and splaying his hands over Sun's hips felt equally important. Westin breathed in—rosemary and oranges, a scent for an older man inclined to be serious, not for a pretty danger like Sun. "Violets for you instead?" he mused, because that scent had drawn Sun's attention even over the smell of hot food when he'd been exhausted, soaking wet, and probably hungry.

"Are you drunk?" Sun demanded of Westin's shoulder. He still hadn't moved away, or asked Westin to, or offered any real challenge to the idea of Westin playing Noble's Pet with him.

That was probably confusion, Westin told himself, or perhaps some pity, though Hely would be annoyed that Westin thought so.

He pulled away, watching Sun stiffen as Westin took the step back to his cushioned seat and half fell into it.

Westin looked up at him with raised eyebrows. "Have you ever known me to get drunk?"

"No." Sun crossed, then uncrossed, his arms. "I've heard stories of you from when you were younger that the others tell me. But you don't get drunk. Not that I've seen."

"Not really. Not anymore." Westin had no idea why any other guards would find old stories about him interesting enough to tell. He didn't get into fights or behave recklessly when drinking. He usually just tipped to the side and fell asleep. "And not around you." Their eyes met. "Not if you're drinking," Westin amended, because he wasn't going to bring up what he imagined of Sun's childhood. "I like to make sure you're all right. And that whoever you're flirting with understands that you have a protector if needed."

"Why are you telling me this?" Sun shot a startled look around the booth. "Is it because we're here? It's this place?" He shook that off. "I don't need a keeper—and you will say that I know you do that and that I allow you to do it because I like it."

"Will I say that?" Westin asked, his heart pounding more than ever. "You knew I watched over you?"

"I knew you watched me," Sun said, turning to stare at the candles. "But it doesn't matter what I thought. I'm not going to empty your purse, West. Especially not now, if you really are retiring."

"Hmm." Westin wondered if he was giving off sparks again. If so, Sun didn't seem to see them.

"You can afford to buy me a bath," Sun allowed, oddly tense. "And a room for yourself, and food, and some tea. Maybe for both of us. But two baths plus this? In *this* inn? I know I tease, but I don't really want to cause trouble. Not for you anyway. I can't be Hely but I can at least manage that much."

Westin set aside the fixation on Hely for later examination. There was only so much he could think about with any sort of clarity with a half-naked Sun before him and several significant possibilities making his blood burn.

"You aren't trouble. Not really. Not to me." Westin was firm. "But you're worth trouble. No matter what else is said in this booth, remember it's a space for truth." At that, Sun raised one eyebrow. Westin nodded. "All right, you're *some* trouble. But nothing

I mind. You might not believe me now, but Hely says I spark at the thought of you, something he's never seen from me before. That's only for you, Sun, and maybe it worries me but I was sitting in this inn, *this* inn, alone, trying to settle my thoughts at the idea of a future that seemed dull and lonely—and still will be, more than likely. Then you came in and nothing was dull anymore. You're worth more to me than anything this inn could offer."

Sun was in Westin's lap, knees on either side of his thighs, his hands in Westin's braid, before Westin had time to worry over whether he should take the words back. He steadied Sun by taking a firm hold of his waist and Sun shoved closer even before Westin had him secure and safe, his mouth hot beneath Westin's ear.

"What did you use?" Sun demanded, his nose in Westin's hair even while his fingers did their best to unravel the braiding. "You smell so fucking good. Months." His voice cracked. "*Months*. Will you tup me right here? I won't cost you anything."

Westin slid a hand up Sun's back to his neck to grip short, damp hair. Sun moved for him without Westin having to tug, tilting his head to bare his throat for Westin to kiss. His skin was still overly warm from the bathwater and unbelievably smooth for someone who lived on the road most of the time.

But he was always so careful with himself. Westin gently kissed several freckles for that. His heart was going to burst no matter what Sun told him. Even if Sun said no, Westin would have this moment.

"You will cost me everything," Westin murmured as he scouted for more freckles to kiss.

Sun stiffened. Westin had sense enough to tighten his hold to keep Sun in his lap, but fortunately, Sun wasn't inclined to fight him over it yet and stayed where he was.

"The truth comes out." Sun hit him with a charming smile. "I'm too much trouble."

"That is not what I mean." Westin exhaled. "I mean I'm dependable, reliable, and strong. Boring," he added in case that wasn't clear. "Responsible." That was to please Hely. "Some people like that. But I'm not remarkable in any way." He held tighter to the bird in his lap. "I accept that you would want me as a friend. I accept that you might pass time with me as lovers do. But it doesn't take much of your attention to spin me around and turn me into a cock-led fool. I'm sure you enjoy that, but that's not all I want."

"Are you trying to flatter me?" Sun asked in a tone so light and thin it was brittle. "Are you being *gentle* with me, Westin?" He laughed and Westin got goosebumps. "You want peace. And you won't find that with me *spinning you around*. It's fine." He squirmed again, not quite fighting to get free although he could have. "It's fine, West. I'll leave you to *Hely*."

"Don't be charming with me." It slipped out, tight and pained, but it made Sun stop. "No." Westin shook his head. "Not that kind of charming. Not the effort to make sure I'll still keep you around—is that why you didn't pick a floral scent for your bath?"

This time when Sun wriggled, Westin let go. Sun pushed backward to rise smoothly to his feet.

Westin looked up. "If I wanted Hely, I would be with Hely." He silently apologized to Hely for the presumption, because Hely's time was his own. "I wanted you the moment you walked in here and I wanted you before then, and you *know* that, so I don't understand why you'd try to pretend. Unless it's to spare my feelings, but I'd rather have the brat telling me off than that. Do you worry that if we aren't fucking, I won't want you around anymore?" Westin gazed up in sudden horror, all the heat leaving him. "Is that why you're here now?"

Sun raised his eyebrows, trying to appear lofty and distant when he should have been snarling. "You think I'm that concerned with keeping you near me that I'd try to charm you into ignoring my faults?"

That wasn't what Westin had said, as Hely might have pointed out. Not at all.

Westin missed the herbal-citrus scent now, if only for the distraction it had provided. He tried to focus on something else instead, the faint spice scent lingering in his hair, the one Sun claimed to like.

"You rushed in here without shoes." Westin almost sounded calm. "Or a shirt. You journeyed to Solace House in a storm when you were going to see me in a day or two anyway." He was as gentle as he could be but Sun's loftiness increased, his chin rising in challenge. Westin inhaled again. "You are going to take another bath tomorrow, and you're going to linger and choose whatever soaps please you because they please *you*. And I am going to pay for it all, because I care about you and I like indulging you. You don't have to try to charm me. I never want that. I didn't make the offer for you to share my room out of any expectation of—"

Sun bent down to press a finger to Westin's mouth. "Shut up."

Westin ignored the warning because Sun might not love him, but he needed to hear more truth between them. "Your only mistake was being rude to Hely. You're lucky Hely found it amusing. Anything else you think you did wrong you only did because that's how we are with each other. And I like that, Sun. I like you. I lo—"

Sun cut him off by taking over Westin's lap for the second time, grabbing Westin's hands and slapping them to his waist before hiding his face at Westin's shoulder. "Look how much trouble I am."

"You're a brat," Westin answered honestly, pleased to hold and pet and stroke bath-warmed skin. "But I get to call you that."

He didn't make it a question, but Sun shivered and pressed harder against him. "I put you through so much. Even now I.... I wasn't *that* rude to Hely. I can tell when people like me, and Hely likes me."

"He said you might have charmed him." *If he hadn't already seen him with Westin.* Westin didn't add that part. "When I find you charming, it's not like how you are with others. Do what you please, brat. But I was charmed when you shook water from your hair like a dog in the street to piss off a beat-of-four and I am just as charmed when you sing lullabies in your sleep."

"I do not do that." It was remarkably haughty for someone rubbing his cheek against Westin's jaw. "Instead of another bath, buy some of whatever soap you used, so you might always smell like this."

"I would only use it if you were coming to visit me." Westin didn't say it without thought, but nonetheless, Sun went as tense as a bowstring.

"If you insist upon going." The cool words would have had more of an impact if Sun hadn't moved on to nuzzling the grays by Westin's temple.

"But will you visit?" That was the question that would have had Westin equally tense if he hadn't had Sun to attend to. "I have trained myself out of expecting things. I don't look for them. Hely," he paused to croon at the grumbling ferret in his lap, "suggested in his way that I might have misunderstood some things for this reason. I will probably continue to do that. So I will ask. And if you could answer, that would be appreciated. Words would help me more than growls, wolfling."

"Words like offering to travel with you?" Sun pulled more of Westin's hair from its braid, tugging and yanking like a nesting bird. He scoffed when the words sank in and Westin twitched. Sun inched back. "You're infuriating, you know." He looked at Westin but then glanced away. "I didn't and don't expect you to care." His chin came up. "But I did expect you to at least notice. And don't *Sunlark* me. I don't want your pity."

"Pity?" Westin was surprised it wasn't a squeak.

Sun glared. "You probably won't need someone at your back to protect you wherever you end up. Wait, where *will* you end up?"

That wasn't a no, even if it also wasn't a yes. Westin had no idea how he'd gone from enjoying a calming pot of tea to waiting at a cliff's edge, but that was Sun. If Westin hadn't wanted to live like this, he would have done something about it long before this moment.

He also hadn't fully explained himself. Sun didn't know what Westin was offering, so how could he know if he wanted it?

Westin pressed his fingertips into Sun's waist both to feel Sun's skin and to help hold Sun if Sun tried to bolt. He breathed in, one last odd inhale of herbs and oranges.

He began as calmly as he was able, treading carefully. "My family land is near here. You could visit on your way to or from the capital, if you cared to. Please accept that I was going to tell you. I've failed in several ways, but I was never going to disappear. I *did* hesitate over how to tell you, partly because I wasn't sure how."

"I suppose that's something." Sun glowered. "Afraid of me?"

Westin had no fear of puppy teeth. The opposite in fact.

"No, my fears were more that you wouldn't care that I was going." He had less than a moment to forestall the fury rising in Sun. "Because that would have hurt almost as much as never seeing you again." Sun tensed under his hands. Westin went on, had to. "You are dear to me, brat, though the fae know I am mostly someone for you to tease."

Sun's hands slowly fell from Westin's hair. "I thought you liked it." His mouth twisted unhappily. "I'm vexing, I know. Hardly *peaceful*."

"Troublesome," Westin admitted. "But I like a little trouble, it turns out. Provided it's not the sort of trouble that requires drawn swords." Doubt was all over Sun's face. Westin reached up to stroke down Sun's nose and then brush his lips before cupping his jaw. "I like you," he said again, holding that stubborn stare, "but I can't do another winter. I realized it not long ago. I was going to try. But I can't. I'm older now—not ancient, but too old for the Outguard and too old for you. I know that but there it is."

Sun flinched away from his hand. Westin let it drop to his side.

Sun smiled with far too much warmth. "Of course, you'd be nice to me now." He flicked a wrist dismissively and made his smile blinding. "You'll at least manage to take care of yourself around your family, won't you? Think of Hely."

"*Lark*." Westin barked it and Sun forgot to smile as their eyes met. "Are you being kind and ignoring my words or do you not understand what is in them?"

The answer was obvious once the question was out. Westin had told Hely that Sun might not know the futures available to him but Westin had forgotten that with Sun on his lap.

"Perhaps I'm too young to understand," Sun returned, waspish.

Westin pushed out a breath. *Sparks* failed to explain why he felt like a cedar consumed by lightning.

Sun's eyes widened. Perhaps he finally saw the sparks too. But if he did, they only made him raise his chin, preparing to be difficult.

"You have many friends," Westin enunciated for him, tone sharp again. "You have a home with the Outguard, for life, if you need it."

"The barracks." Sun flicked his wrist again.

"A *home*." Westin was firm on that too. "They love you. And there, you will find better men than me to tease and worry over."

"You really are a jackass," Sun hissed, and Westin was so lost to him, because the insult allowed him to breathe. Sun shoved Westin's chest without any force. "You can just say you don't want me. I get it. I'm small. I'm trouble. Others didn't want me and they were nothing compared to you."

Westin didn't know what he was feeling. He certainly wasn't thinking clearly. "You said I was too soft."

"I like soft!" Sun had either forgotten he could get up whenever he wanted or had no real desire to. "I like *you*! And you like *peace* and calm, older, handsome men who have manners, but it's me you're staring at now! Me!"

"You," Westin agreed, before taking Sun's face in his hands to kiss his furious, sulky mouth.

Sun pushed forward, his chest pressed to Westin's, his hands buried in Westin's hair. He rose to his knees to kiss the breath from Westin, whined when Westin dared to want to breathe, then was back on Westin before Westin could do more than gasp. *Hungers for you*, Westin heard in Hely's voice, and felt the reality of it in how Sun shivered for Westin's hands sliding up his spine and bit his way into Westin's mouth as if he thought Westin might deny him if he gave Westin even a moment to think.

Westin took hold of Sun's hair again, tugging Sun from him to find air at last, but offering gentler, deliberate kisses before Sun could do more than clutch at him; catching his breath was far less important than assuaging the brat's fears. He forced their kissing to slow, lingering over Sun's mouth because it was so beautiful and he liked how Sun gave in and gentled for him despite his hunger. Then, with another slow, heated kiss, he looked into Sun's eyes. Endless black *need* stared back at him.

"I'm here," he reminded Sun, awe letting him stay light in the face of so much desire. "I want you. I've got you."

Sun pushed forward again, fighting Westin's hold on his hair to kiss his way up Westin's jaw, then sucking a desperate bruise beneath his ear. "You're not inside me," he said, with teeth. "As though I didn't bathe for that. Must I pay you to have you?" Perhaps he meant it as a demand or playful coaxing, but there was nothing light in his next words. "*Months*, Wes,*" spilled from him, and no matter how he hid his face, Westin heard the truth.

They had only been kissing for moments, Westin reflected dizzily, but moved his hands down to grab Sun's backside and pull Sun tighter to him. Sun's breathing grew fast and high, close to whining again. Westin squeezed hard with some desperation of his own and turned his head to find Sun's mouth and claim it.

He spared half a thought, half a moment, to grab the hilt of the knife Sun had tucked into the back of his pants and toss the weapon to the other bench. Sun might not have taken the time to completely dry himself, but arming himself would have been reflex.

One danger handled, Westin returned both of his hands to Sun, sweeping his palms over his orange-scented skin until Sun stopped whining altogether and shivered as he let Westin touch him.

"Hard?" Westin whispered, sliding a touch between Sun's legs. He murmured an apology for the shock that went through Sun, but forcibly returned Sun's hands to his shoulders when Sun tried to reach between them.

"Of course I am!" Sun nearly snarled it, then caught himself and glanced away. Then he gave Westin a heated look, face tipped down, lashes flicking up so their eyes would meet. His lips were rosy, wet, and very close. "Are you going to make me wait? Or should I go find someone else?"

He wasn't going anywhere, not if Westin responded in kind. That was how it always went, but it had never made as much sense as it did now.

Westin inched forward to speak against that pout. "Don't I always give you what you want?" He slipped his hands into the back of Sun's pants and discovered Sun hadn't paused to put on any smalls either. He kneaded hot, bare skin, enjoying Sun's long shudder. "I wanted you to linger in the bath. I liked thinking about it, even with those cuffs."

"These cuffs?" Sun echoed innocently while pushing his backside into Westin's hands. He turned his head for a moment, displaying his jewelry and looking sly when Westin kissed his neck. "You don't like them?"

"Brat." It was too strong, too loud, but Sun's smile grew. That meant the whole inn could hear them and Westin wouldn't care. Sun tipped his head up, displaying himself or those cursed cuffs. Not even Westin stroking a fingertip over his hole could entirely wipe the smug pleasure from his face. "You like them, I get it," Westin told him, too caught up in an evening of revelations to spend time wondering at his harsh tone.

Even if he'd wanted to, Sun gave him no chance.

"I could get gold," he murmured, watching Westin through slitted eyes. "You said I could."

Westin let his voice be rough. "Are you asking me if you're handsome enough or if you're charming enough?"

Sun spread his knees, slipping down a little further onto Westin's trapped cock while offering himself to Westin's hands. His gaze was steady and serious. "*You'd* look good in gold, West. You'd look so good."

Westin laughed without meaning to.

Sun's eyes narrowed. He rose, and then Westin was shoved back and wrestled down. It helped that Westin put up no fight, only returning his hands to Sun's hips to steady him as he wound up on his back with Sun splayed on top of him. The benches in Solace House booths were wide for a reason, but one wrong move and one or both of them would topple to the floor. Sun was not light, either; even wiry muscle had heft. Westin gripped him tight to keep Sun from falling, flattered that Sun took it for granted that he would.

Sun's hips were pressed to his and his hands were on the cushioned seat by Westin's head—in Westin's hair, actually, although Westin could have pushed away if he'd wanted to.

He did not want to. Sun glared down at him. He was hard and Westin was on his way to match him there. The glare only made it worse.

"I *said* you would look good in gold." The reprimand was heated. Then Sun was kissing him again, holding Westin still to have his mouth how he pleased.

Westin's hands flexed. He didn't have to pull Sun down against his cock, Sun was already rocking against him, small, impatient motions at odds with his coaxing tone.

"It would suit you," he breathed against Westin's jaw and then his neck, all the while grinding down against Westin until Westin was hard too. Then he slowed and it felt purposeful. Maybe his plan was to leave Westin too riled to think clearly. "If I were a noble and you were mine, you would smell like this and look like this all the time, and I'd cover you in gold." He scraped his teeth over Westin's neck and then slipped his hands down to pull at Westin's shirt. "Cuffs and necklaces. Rings. I'd draped them from your cock, your chest, your waist, everywhere. You'd look so good and all others would know you were mine."

"I'm not the pet here," Westin reminded him, hoarse and confused, but pushed down on Sun's hips to keep Sun where he was, then pushed up with a little groan when Sun responded by rubbing against him.

"*I'm* the pet," Sun crowed into Westin's neck. "And you're so pretty. Silver and gold," he added nonsensically, a hitch in the words. "Dark and lovely. I'm your pet. Your pet. Only me." Shivers wracked through him as though he was close to finishing.

It had to be their time apart or the strange fantasy of Westin in gold, but his brat was aching and that couldn't stand. Westin stopped, stroking up and down Sun's back before slipping his hands into Sun's pants again to cup pleasing handfuls. He squeezed and spread Sun's backside apart as much as Sun's clothing would allow. Sun began to whine again.

"That's all?" Sun demanded, shaking against him. "You won't undress me or fuck me?"

He could undress himself, but that wasn't what he wanted. The demand was really a request, his defiance a plea.

"Sweet boy." Westin sought his mouth and then his jaw and neck to leave them wet and stinging, all the while gripping hot, smooth skin to make Sun shudder and hitch and rock down. He debated getting up to get Sun naked or to get oils or towels from one of the cabinets, but didn't want to take his hands from Sun.

"Later," he promised, teasing Sun with a dry finger and enjoying how he squirmed, "in our room." The hiccup in Sun's breathing was worth Westin's small moment of fear at claiming the room for them both. "There's no need to rush."

The wriggling brat on top of him whined again. "*Months*, West, and then months more, always. Always months without you. And then..."

"And then you can find me again, whenever you like." Westin was a cock-led old fool.

Sun raised his head to stare at Westin with dark eyes in a flushed face. "And I just come begging to you?"

Westin hauled Sun against him, rocking up at the same time to watch need take over Sun's expression. "It would make me happy to see you and to have you make use of me. It has always made me happy." There was more danger, more fear, his heart seizing in his chest when Sun went still, but Westin had been too much of a coward already. "It would make me happiest if you never left. I don't expect that, but you should know it."

Something flickered through Sun's face. Then he looked away, concealing whatever it was. "I'm a very good fuck," he said in a hot, cutting tone before smiling.

Westin caught a glimpse of that bitter smile and resigned himself to fucking sense into Sun in this booth with the customers of Solace House outside and scandalized because Sun could not be quiet.

He wrapped his arms around Sun and moved Sun with strength and speed and knowledge of how quick Sun could move in return. He rolled them both over, then was off the bench and looking down at a startled, glaring Sun.

"Brat," Westin called, tender, "you make me do things I would never ordinarily consider."

"Things you regret?" Sun panted, lying on his back as Westin had left him, his pants inching down, his cock stiff and obvious beneath the cloth.

Westin put a hand to the top of the seat and bent down to kiss him, shocked and pleased anew when Sun instantly stretched to meet him, lips supple and clinging. "No," Westin whispered to him, petting his handsome face and giving him another kiss. "Although I'll owe Hely so much." He stroked Sun's frown before it could fully form and then straightened up. "Roll over, brat, and my cock is yours."

Sun had no reason to look so surprised. He'd been loud enough with Westin to upset an innkeeper used to all kinds of noise. He knew what he could get Westin to do.

But his surprise was momentary. Then he was smug. "It *is* mine," he agreed, before turning to put his face to the cushioned seat. "I'll show your Hely that." He had one knee on the bench and one foot on the floor and splayed his fingers as if he was trying to grip the cushion. Westin reached for his belt, then tugged Sun's pants down to his knees without removing them.

The startled noise Sun made when Westin went into a cabinet for supplies was gratifying, as were the snippy remarks that followed it.

"Oh, I see you know where everything is. Is that what Hely likes? Or maybe you enjoy variety. How would I know? It's not as if you told me what you do here."

With someone else, Westin could have assumed they were asking for a spanking, something he'd never considered because as far as he knew, Sun did not particularly enjoy pain and had never demanded such things from him. But perhaps it wasn't about pain with Sun, but what he could get Westin to do. Or perhaps it was about Sun knowing he was misbehaving and trusting Westin to do what he felt was right. *Some people are good,* Sun had said, no matter how much he pushed them.

The thought made Westin pause with oil all over his palms as he warmed it.

"Mostly, when I'm here, I drink tea and enjoy a nice bath and a talk with a close friend." Westin paused again for the grumbled "Mostly" that followed that. "You look lovely this way," Westin observed quietly, "but I do feel as if you are asking for correction. Or perhaps testing to see if I will offer it. I've never done that before," he added, heated to consider it. It wasn't the idea of hurting Sun; it was the thought that Sun might want to know where the line was, that he might want Westin to provide the line.

"Correction?" Sun echoed without any confusion, his face still down, ass still up and on offer. "What is it I've done? *You're* the one with the secret Solace House lover."

"Correction suited to a brat." Westin stood behind him, enjoying the view, then stopped at a memory. "Am I really the only one allowed to call you that?"

Goosebumps appeared over Sun's back, followed by a shiver.

"So?" The word was defiance and challenge, but Sun had tremors in his voice too.

Westin slid a touch over the curves of Sun's backside, then spread them to get Sun shiny with oil. Sun wasn't fully relaxed but he wasn't tense, either. Westin also wasn't as slow as he could have been. Sun shuddered and bent his head and said not a word about it. If anything, he pushed into it.

Westin chose his words carefully. "Did you do this to yourself in the bath, brat?"

"Thinking of you," Sun admitted after a moment, either needing to focus to speak or annoyed at being asked. "I wanted to be ready."

"And you wanted to please me." Westin hoped his disbelief wasn't too obvious. "So you chose a scent you thought would entice me and worked yourself open, and thought of me, or of this—of getting me to do this exactly where we are so that Hely and everyone else would know I'm yours."

"Wes…"

"Jealous enough to make a scene in the middle of an inn—again," Westin added, his voice rough though he was far from angry. He did wonder what had occurred in the last inn they'd stayed in that had made the brat decide the entire countryside needed to hear Westin fucking him, but that was a question for another time.

"I wanted to be ready," Sun explained again, trembling too much to be convincingly snotty.

"Because it's been months, and my cock is yours, so why wouldn't you prepare yourself to take it?" Westin soothed away objections before they could happen, if Sun could even have managed any once Westin began to ready him properly. Westin was patient and thorough and perhaps just mean enough about it to have shocked Hely. He took his time because he enjoyed the task and because Sun had been squirming and fretting in a bath meant to melt such worries away and he needed to learn he didn't have to do that.

This was correction.

"I'm ready," Sun said after long moments of Westin spreading oil but not pushing in.

"You're not," Westin argued, but decided to finally indulge him.

Sun tensed for the first press inside, then gave way all at once as he always did, body heavy and hot around Westin's fingers. No fear or worry, only ever hunger that would swallow all that Westin had. Westin pressed in to the knuckle and stopped there, holding still until Sun squirmed again.

"What did you think about in the bath?" Westin wondered, sparing a hand to hold Sun in place. "Me having you on one of the tables outside?"

Sun snarled something possibly not meant for Westin to hear.

"Ah." Westin was briefly stunned. "Hely said so, but I didn't believe it."

"*Hely.*" Another snarl.

"Hely," Westin agreed, resuming his work at a pace that would not suit Sun's impatience, but not letting Sun do more than wriggle and complain.

"Does Hely like it this slow?" The more outraged Sun was, the slower Westin went.

"*Months*, and I'm no delicate inn-blossom. Be honest and fuck me."

That was too much, too wounded.

Westin pinched the inside of Sun's thigh before resuming his careful work over the sound of Sun's startled, even shocked, gasp. He waited for further complaints but apparently the pinch had settled his boy.

Sun was a gift, exactly as Hely had said. Westin could offer himself in return, for whatever he was worth.

"I'm yours whenever you need me. You know that. I know you do. Brat." Westin emphasized that with the sudden push of three fingers and Sun scrabbled at the cushion and turned his head to pant.

"*West*," he complained, then, "Wes," the softer name, the one heard much less often.

"Lark-in-my-hand," Westin answered, curling his fingers to make Sun's knees give out. Sun moaned loud enough to be heard beyond the curtain. "Will you come visit me? Demand this from me?"

"West," Sun complained again, attempting to crawl back up onto his knees only for Westin to stroke him inside again, firm and repetitive, while Sun jerked and failed to get a good hold on the cushion. His rising gasps were beautiful, announcing as much as the shivers tearing through him that he was again close to peaking.

Westin could make Sun finish this way, deeper and messier but ultimately unsatisfying because it wasn't what Sun was currently after. Sun wanted Westin in him, pressed close and saying his name. He thought of Westin when Westin was gone, and desired him, and trusted him this much. They could build a life on that, if the brat wanted.

Westin wanted it so much that he didn't care how foolish he was for offering. "Or you could stop worrying about Hely or any others and come with me, stay with me. I'll be yours. I *am* yours, brat. That's already true and has been for some time now."

Sun made a small, broken sound as his knees gave out again. Westin removed his fingers in order to take Sun by the waist and move him up and over. Sun's eyes met his, greedy and frightened, wholly dark and focused on Westin, and there was a stir in Westin's chest, a rush of beat-of-four blood that had never been so strong before.

Take, it said, and even terrified, Westin liked it. He liked everything about Sun, even the risk to his heart. He tugged Sun's pants the rest of the way off and tossed them to the other bench on top of Sun's knife. He pushed Sun's knees up and half kneeled on the bench, and then he was sinking into Sun while Sun shuddered and sucked in breaths and tried to pull Westin in to force him deeper. *Sun would take all of him*, Westin thought, over and over. All of him, until Westin was balls deep and still, and even then, Sun would try to get more.

The space between them was hot, the position uncomfortable. Westin rocked into him with their faces close. Sun's gaze was almost fae-black in the dim light and fixed on Westin. His mouth was open, his hands tangled in Westin's hair.

"Lark." Westin exhaled it, sweeping a hand along the outside of Sun's thigh and then down beneath Sun to haul Sun against him, bending Sun nearly in half to meet his hips with every short thrust.

Sun gripped Westin's shoulders and a handful of what remained of Westin's braid and called Westin his private name for him clear enough to be heard at the bar. "Wes. Wes, *please.*" With his voice hitching and the breath squeezed from him, and Westin doing all the work. Westin panted over his ear and pulled Sun's legs up higher, tighter, and Sun made a stuttering, wet sound and yanked Westin's hair in his fist as he finished.

That was another order; Sun liked to feel a fuck long after the act was over. Westin thrust into him a few more times to make Sun's cries pained and pleased, and then pulled out to grind into the mess and add his own to it. Sun liked that too, Westin's seed all over him. He liked Westin to spill inside but he sometimes begged for the mess.

Better than a cuff for showing who Sun had been with, or so the long-denied beat-of-four inside Westin insisted as Westin groaned and reached down to coax another few pearly drops onto Sun, and watched Sun's muscles flutter beneath the spill, a sight far lovelier than gold.

He still had one of Sun's thighs pushed nearly to Sun's chest. Sun was breathing hard but not objecting, although he would soon. Westin thought the common room had grown louder, but it might have been the blood still pounding in his ears mingling with distant shocked murmurs.

He brushed a kiss over Sun's forehead, the damp hair and the traces of sweat, and hoped he didn't appear too anxious when Sun's eyes came open.

"We should eat soon," Westin heard himself saying, which, though true, was not what was in his heart. "If you still want to stay with me after, the bed will fit two."

Sun narrowed his eyes, which suggested some displeasure as though he wasn't catching his breath or covered in seed. The hint of color along his cheekbones was probably also at the back of his neck, bringing out the freckles he disliked so much but which he often allowed Westin to kiss, one by one.

Secret, stolen moments, Westin had always believed. Times when a recently-pleasured Sun allowed Westin to be foolish and tolerated his affection.

That was not the case, and if it ever had been, Sun had long since come to expect those moments. Even to look forward to them, Westin suspected, and released a deep sigh. Sun had trained Westin to please him, but Westin had done some training too, even if he hadn't intended to.

"A bath in the morning," he continued, wishing he'd brought enough with him to pay for two nights. "Violets for you? Gardenias? Roses? It's not jewelry, but…"

Sun slapped a tired hand over his mouth. "Will you be with me in the bath?"

"Not if it smells like roses," Westin answered honestly. "But I could be in the room, if that's what you're asking."

Sun pulled his hand away. "You enjoyed thinking about me having the bath. That's what you said." He observed Westin intently. "If you're with me, you could watch. Although, then—" Whatever he'd been about to say, he forgot as he moved his leg and winced.

Westin was off him in a heartbeat, reaching for a towel before gently helping Sun lower his legs and get comfortable. The brat lay back with his thighs open and his posture loose, allowing—expecting—Westin to clean him with his chin ever so slightly in the air.

"West," Sun called after a while of Westin straightening his clothes and setting the towel aside and *not* thinking about the world beyond the curtain. He wasn't ready to leave yet. But Sun must not have been either, because he curled a finger to get Westin closer, then patted the spot on the bench next to him.

Westin sat with his hands on his knees, glancing briefly and with some small despair to his knitting, which had been shoved to the floor. But he forgot it again quickly, startled by Sun curling up along the rest of the bench and using one of Westin's thighs for a pillow. Westin snatched his hands out of the way only just in time.

"Tired?" he probed gently. "You didn't have to travel hard to find me. You know I'd never ask that of you." Sun reached up, found Westin's hand, and dragged it down to his head. Westin nodded in understanding of what Sun apparently didn't want to say. "You needed this?" He clucked his tongue when Sun tensed and began to gently scratch Sun's scalp to make that tension go away. "I'm sorry." He scratched and soothed and petted while their heartbeats slowed and their breathing grew even.

"You're too nice." Sun was very quiet. "Always resolving the problems of others. What about you?"

Westin paused, then lightly stroked down the back of Sun's neck to one faintly freckled shoulder. "I didn't say what I said to appease you. I said it because it's what I wanted. I'm perhaps as soft as you think I am, but even I wouldn't swear myself to someone simply to be nice."

Sun rolled over to stare at Westin for several tense moments. "Swear yourself?" he asked at last, even quieter than before. The rain was just audible.

Westin pulled his hand away and was only mildly comforted when Sun reached for it to make Westin put it back.

"Forgive me." Discomfort had Westin glancing away, to the curtain that held back the rest of the world. "I've never asked before—never even considered asking before. I got ahead of myself, didn't I? I keep trying to tell you what a fool I am…"

"Shut up," Sun interrupted. He placed Westin's hand over his ribs. "Keep going."

Westin gestured apologetically with his free hand. "I had a regular lover and didn't realize. A lover who offered to stay with me. Who has chased me down more than once, from the sound of it. Who initiated everything between us, every time. I have much to make up for if you give me a chance. And I cannot even offer jewelry. Well, I suppose I could, although it wouldn't be gold. Perhaps someday, but certainly not now. You're not only interested in that, but you should have it if you want it. You're worthy of it. And if some other beat-of-four can offer you that, then…"

"What in the name of the fae are you talking about, West?" Sun frowned up at him.

The snap returned some of Westin's sense. He hadn't babbled like that around a lover since he'd been younger than Sun. He inhaled and let the scent of their fucking mingled with cress spice and orange and rosemary be his focus and not the fears and desires and need filling his chest.

He exhaled.

"If you wanted, if not today then someday, I would marry you, Sun."

Sheltered from the candles and the hint of light from the common room by the bench and Westin's body, Sun's face was in shadow, his eyes wide and near black again. His lips were pressed tight together and no words escaped them.

Westin nodded because he needed to do something and he couldn't yet get up and walk away. "I want you to have a place you can call home if you don't like the barracks, and to know you can count on me to be there for you. And though I didn't admit this to myself until tonight, when I'm traveling and alone, I look for you and am disappointed when you aren't there. Of course, you're also welcome to visit me or stay with me even if you don't imagine our hands tied together. But you should know it's a future that's available to you. I'm… I'm available to you, lark, whenever you need." He cleared his throat. "But I know you will be on the road a great deal, and I wouldn't expect you to think only of me." Most marriages, when they occurred, did not demand that, but Westin wanted to be clear. "I know you're fond of me but I won't have you burdened by what I've realized is in my heart."

"In your heart?" Sun echoed faintly, then scrambled to sit up. He looked around the booth and Westin had the wild thought that Sun was hoping Hely would appear. "*In your heart?*" he charged again, rounding back on Westin. "Available?" His eyes were huge. "*Marry?*"

"It's an option," Westin explained, *almost* reasonably. Sun wouldn't be fooled but a stranger might have been.

"An *option*?" Sun's voice went a little higher.

"You can say no," Westin continued while that put-off and tamped-down stirring in his chest began to grow and deepen.

"*No*?" Sun didn't howl it, but the murmurs from the common room paused as though the sound had carried. "West, you.... West." He quieted with his hands at his cheeks and his gaze on Westin. "Are you drunk?" he asked again, very low.

"No, lark." Westin reached for him and got a lapful of warm, naked Sun, who pressed his face to Westin's shoulder and kept it there. Westin settled and steadied him, his arms around Sun's back. "I'm retiring, and I treasure you so much that I want you to know the truth before I go. Which Hely helped me realize—don't growl."

"And the truth is that you are 'available to me?'" Sun didn't raise his head but the growl remained in his voice. "Am I not available to you? So obviously that everyone in the guard knows it and your handsome friend too? I rode here for you. In a storm." That was added with a hint of a pout and Westin nuzzled Sun's hair without thought.

"You did," he agreed.

"In a *storm*, West," Sun said again, more than a hint of a pout about him now. He angled his head so he could look up at Westin. "I was wet and cold." He shivered to demonstrate. "And you asked why I was here."

"You drank that tea for me." Westin was warmed by the memory. "You tolerate my fears so well, Sun."

Sun blinked. "*Tolerate*? Oh yes. Because you are a burden to me. And I am to find others on the road while I'm away from you, my proposed husband." He smiled with teeth and turned his head again, letting the cuffs find the light. "When I find all these others, should I try for gold?"

Words stuck in Westin's throat. The stirring in his chest returned. He closed his eyes. "You deserve gold."

"Hmm." Sun was very pleased about something. He wriggled in Westin's arms, settling firmly into Westin's lap before humming again. Westin opened his eyes. Sun's gaze was intent on him. "Too generous," he purred. "You need someone to be selfish for you."

Westin thought he was doing quite well with Sun's not-quite rejection but some hurt made his voice tart. "Oh, do I?"

"Yes." Sun was confident, his head tipped up, his lips curved. "Your Hely thinks so too." He turned again, letting his jewelry glint inches from Westin's face. His voice was silky and vicious. "If you don't like these cuffs, you should say so. That's what you'd tell me to do. *Use your words.*" He added that in a mocking tone, all the while watching Westin with dark, dark eyes.

"I am not territorial," Westin insisted, the lie making his voice rough. "Someone *should* give you nice things and care about you." He meant that even with his heart pounding and his palms itching. "But...." He barely stopped himself in time.

Sun reached for one of Westin's hands and pulled it to his neck, just below his ear, before letting go. "But? This is a space for the truth, West. You said so."

"They're gorgeous on you," Westin admitted hoarsely. "But I don't like seeing them." He stopped again, mouth open in horror. "I won't tell you to take them off."

"Just take them off, then," Sun suggested before Westin could go on. He inched his chin up even higher, then turned away, his eyes briefly closed, his breathing unsteady. He wet his lips. "If you dislike seeing them so much, tear them off me."

"But they matter to you." Westin forced himself to say it.

Sun only shrugged, which might or might not have been a lie. "Someone who likes me offered to buy them for me, and I thought that I could have them, and perhaps sell them later if I ever needed money. And I look good in them, don't I? And then I also thought, maybe if I wear gifts from someone else, Wes will notice." Westin would swear his heart stuttered but it might have been the slight hitch in Sun's breathing. "And you did notice. And you don't like them." Oh, he was pleased with himself now, all the while gazing at Westin with a challenge in his expression. "Will you tell me to take them off? Or will you simply do it yourself?"

He shivered at the first glancing touch against the shell of his ear but otherwise kept still when Westin slid the lowest cuff free. The brat wanted him to and Westin wanted it more than he could ever say. Maybe that was *why* Sun wanted it, although Westin didn't think so, not when Sun tipped his head to prompt Westin to take the next one as well. Westin was gentle. He would never tear them off, but Sun had known that when he'd said it.

Maybe it was that one of the candles was failing, leaving them in worse light, but Sun's eyes were endless again. Hungry, as if Westin taking care with the cuffs was better than him ripping them away and now Sun was going to demand even more from him.

"Oh," Westin said aloud, giving Sun every treat he could think of. "I don't like seeing them on you," he told Sun again to make Sun flush prettily. "Especially when you weren't wearing a scarf from me." Many would have been surprised to hear Westin handing out challenges almost as Sun did while slowly stripping some other man's gifts from Sun's body. "Despite the rain," he added. "And the cold."

Sun's laugh was startled. He glanced up with more hunger. "Your last one blew off over a bridge a while back, on the windiest day I've ever seen. I was hoping for a replacement before this winter...." He trailed off, leading and impertinent. "Is that one meant for me?"

Westin did not generally knit designs into his work. His scarves were plain compared to jewelry, and yet Sun's wriggle said Westin's answer had better be yes.

"It is now." With his palm full of jewelry, the stirring inside Westin had calmed enough for him to leave the final cuff at Sun's nose in place, although he tucked the rest of the cuffs into his pocket instead of handing them to Sun. He would eventually, but for now, they were out of sight. Sun must have approved, because he closed his eyes to allow Westin to rub the places where the cuffs had pinched. His ear was bare now. For Westin, although really for Sun.

For both of them, Westin reasoned, with faint worry at what his family might think of that.

"I'm not normally one to care about territory," Westin rationalized out loud. "I can't be. But I do care for what's mine, that is true. What is the family's," he added, to be fair, but then sighed heavily. "What is mine. Not that I would ever demand...." He fell to silence when Sun turned to look at him directly, eyebrows raised. "I can't be that interesting." It slipped from him in disbelief.

He got sulky attitude. "I'm too young to know better?"

"Urgh." The inarticulate noise would have shocked Westin on any other day. Tonight, it was just one more discovery about himself. "Brat." The brat smiled with pleasure to hear that. Westin nearly made the noise again. "I meant that I am...." He suspected that if he claimed to be boring, Sun would gesture to the curtain and all the people who had heard them in here. "I am only like this with you," Westin tried, then realized that was not a strong argument either. "But that would still not be enough for someone as lively as you. That's what I meant. I don't expect to be your one-and-only."

Again, he fell silent, watching Sun stare at him and then look away, his chin still raised high, his eyebrows still up. Waiting.

"Oh." Westin wondered if he was blushing. He was too old to only now realize all the things he wanted and how much he wanted them—and how he was allowed to want them. Sun had claimed Westin's cock for himself, but Westin hadn't considered the rest of him to also be part of that claim. "Do you want me to be your one-and-only?"

Sun turned back to him, all attitude. "Does Hely share?"

"Do you?" Westin pressed, a thrilling sort of greed in his blood. A dangerous thing to feel and yet he didn't run from it. "You may be a lark in my hand but not in a cage, and...." He waited a moment when Sun scoffed but then repeated himself, hardening his voice. "*Not* in a cage. No matter how much you pout or look at me like that. But," Westin cupped Sun's cheek, "in my hand. There would only room for you there. I never thought to be a one-and-only, but I'm not the sort to keep both hands full anyway."

Sun gave him another crisp look of challenge.

"But you already demand that," Westin realized, warm with relief and growing pleasure, "both of my hands full with you. That's what you like." He nearly purred it, limbs unexpectedly heavy with contentment. He saw the sulk beginning to form around Sun's lips and warded it off with a kiss. "If you wanted to put chains of gold around my cock, brat, I won't stop you. I told you it was yours and then gave it to you. Right here, for Hely and others to hear. That was the point, was it not?"

Sun slid against him hot as melted candlewax, his face back at Westin's shoulder. He released a shaky breath and clutched Westin's waist. "Mine."

Westin wondered if he was meant to hear, it was said so quietly. Thunder rumbled somewhere far away.

Sun spoke again before Westin could ask.

"Are you sure you want me in your home with your family? All those children your sister has, with me around?" Sun said it as though he didn't know lullabies because one of his first tasks at a very young age had been to watch over village children younger than him. "Your mother who sends you letters that wait for you at the barracks, all about your business and what your father has been up to. What?" He pulled back to give Westin an accusing look. "You speak of them often. I listen to you."

"You do, don't you." Westin did not ask.

"I always listen to you." Sun's lower lip trembled on the verge of a pout before he put his cheek to Westin's shoulder. The sulk stayed in his voice. "You don't listen to me."

"Brat." Westin kissed the top of his head and smiled like the sapwit he was. "I listen to you but perhaps I wasn't paying attention to what you meant. I didn't think you, well, anyone, but especially you, could mean it if they said that they will go where I go. But you did say it, and I'm sorry I didn't understand."

He expected a snide comment about how the words could not have been more plain. He got Sun pushing out a long, pained sigh.

"You're *good*."

"Too good?" Westin prompted after a moment, unclear if this was like being "too generous."

Sun shook his head. He continued to cling to Westin, but finally offered the complaint Westin had previously expected. "I would ride with you no matter where you go. I was very clear, West. I was... I was too clear. I didn't like that."

Demand next time, Westin nearly said, because possibly the asking was what had confused him. But even without Hely, he had the sense to keep that unsaid. Anyway, he hoped there wouldn't be a next time.

"I will try to do better when you visit me. I've wanted to bring you for a while, though it will be dull for you. We largely farm, although there is some business elsewhere, which is more of what I do. My mother hasn't been interested in that for some time, and I'm traveling or in the capital anyway."

"You were going to bring me home to meet your family?" Sun made a funny sound. "Before all of this?"

"I was going to invite you, if I ever got the nerve." Westin's cowardice was still bothersome. "I think I was worried you'd say no, and then I'd be forced to confront how much I wanted you to visit. If you visit now," something Sun still had not agreed to, "and you didn't mind it, the offer remains for you to stay there. If you need to, or perhaps during the worst of the winter months, for me and my worries."

"I go the longest without seeing you in the winter." Sun reached up to card his fingers through Westin's hair, unraveling the last of the braid before flinging the tie elsewhere. "And the whole time I know you're afraid. I don't like it." That was a declaration. "I offered to travel with you, stay with you. I said I'd go with you, always. I said that, West." That was a pout. "That hasn't changed. I can work with you. Farming, you said?"

"As well as some other land and business matters. Dull, to many."

"I like dull." It was said slyly.

Westin was strangely not offended. "Brat."

Sun kissed the side of Westin's throat before continuing to pull his hair. "You said too much peace was boring."

"I did say that," Westin agreed absently. "That doesn't mean... ah, Sun, there's something I need to tell you before you decide on any visits."

"*Visits*." Sun scoffed again. "Well, go on. If you can only tell your secrets in Solace House, then you should get on with it so I don't have to drag you back here." He sniffed. "Hely would be too pleased."

Stroking Sun's back to calm him was reflex. So was tightening his hold to prevent Sun from darting away.

"Lyeth is not my entire name." Westin nuzzled a frozen Sun for what was hopefully not the last time. At the clenching of the hands in his hair, telling him that Sun had understood what hadn't been said, Westin continued, quickly. "Corilyeth is a hindrance in my work. It's an embarrassment around other nobles and yet drags me into noble business. I rarely tell anyone unless I'm back in the family territory."

When Sun pushed against his chest, Westin allowed it. He deserved Sun's narrow-eyed stare.

"Are you the landlord here?" Sun demanded, then gasped. "Does Hely know? He knew before me?"

"Sun." Westin gathered Sun's hands and brought them up to kiss them, a gesture he'd seen apologetic husbands do and never once thought he'd be one of them. "We are... well, the land the inn is on is ours, conditionally. It depends on other nobles getting greedy or the ruler doing so, though rulers have thankfully have been inclined to peace for years now. Nobles grow ambitious and it only leads to trouble. Which is not what we are after. Not trouble as nobles know it." He kissed Sun's fingers again. "Bless the current queen for being peaceful and may all our future rulers continue to be so."

"So, yes he did know before me," Sun summed up.

"My mother is The Corilyeth," Westin answered, then hesitated. "For now. *She* would be the landlord, if you insisted. My sister handles most of the land management. But yes, Hely knows. All the locals know. It wasn't only Hely. We're not rich as many noble families are. I can't offer you that. We have no desire for conquest or pleasing rulers. We farm, and do some business, and maintain an old estate, and do not even really have sworn guards, except for a few kept around because they are older. They were mostly for pride anyway. The heads of noble families often travel with sworn guards, even lesser families. As for anything else, I personally have my remaining Outguard pay. Although, with my sister not inclined to diplomacy," or tact, Westin silently apologized to Besse but it was true, "or palace goings on, when my mother chooses to finally rest," Westin tried not to sigh at the rising color in Sun's face, "*I* will be The Corilyeth. But my money is yours. That is, I will use it to spoil you as best as I can. I can be selfish."

"You can't," Sun protested, but weakly, his mind clearly on other matters. "*This is why you lend others money and never ask for it back. Oh, Westin.*"

"We are content with what we have," Westin insisted, repeating what the family believed and had said to each other long before he'd been born. "*I* have always been content with what I had. Until you. You made me want more. It worried me."

"Worried you like the cold worries you?" Sun was among the sharpest and cleverest of the outguards.

"I'm territorial about you," Westin confessed, basking in what the admission did to Sun. "It makes me feel like a beat-of-four."

"You *are* a beat-of-four," Sun reminded him without mercy.

"Yes." Westin breathed out but it didn't calm him. "I can be selfish. In one area, I can."

"With me." Sun shimmied his pleasure at that and then slid back down as if intending to use Westin as a pillow again. Instead, he draped himself over Westin's lap, his chin propped up in his hands, his ass on display, and wriggled when Westin settled his hands on the backs of his thighs. "I've never thought of marriage," he said with his face hidden. "I think you'd regret marrying me, in time."

He paused.

Westin opened his mouth, then reconsidered the challenge for what it was and put a hand over the curve of Sun's backside. That backside had been offered to him for a reason, although Westin still did not feel inclined to spank, and if he did, it would not be in a booth for a whole inn to hear.

But the brat was testing him, so Westin spread Sun's cheeks enough to push two fingers back into his slick body, and Sun gasped in a gratifying way and tried to shift his knees apart.

Westin held him still and pressed in again, seeking and finding where Sun was sensitive from their tupping and stroking with firm pressure. Sun wriggled, then squirmed. He panted and turned his head to glare up at Westin.

"And yet," Westin said thoughtfully, hot and aroused and wound up in ways that would make Sun proud, "I think you'll say yes anyway, if only to keep me away from Hely. I am yours, am I not? You can't trust Hely with me. That's what you said."

Sun groaned and turned his head away again.

"I have no problem with Hely," he puffed out, then jerked away from Westin's fingers only to shove himself back down on them and shudder. "Wes," he said weakly. "It's terrible. It's so much. Don't stop."

"You haven't answered me," Westin reminded him, and slipped in a third finger with beat-of-four impulses stirring in his chest again. It *was* terrible, he silently agreed, and yet shared Sun's desire to keep going.

Sun allowed it, shaking but somehow pleased by it all.

"What I think you really need is someone to watch your back." Sun paused every few words to let a whine escape. "To travel with you when you resolve disputes, or go to the palace, or—West." Sun tried and failed to get his knees apart. He would be demanding cock again soon unless Westin got him to spill over himself and the cushions by continuing this correction. "You should have a sworn gua-*ard*." Sun's voice rose when Westin began to press with steady, regular pressure. "Are you...? I *will* be your guard, Westin. I *will* protect you, even if I am also your pet." He dropped his head to the cushion to pant. "Are you going to fuck me again?"

"You'll be sore." But if Sun wanted it, then yes, he would.

"So I can feel it even when you're gone," Sun said. "Only you won't be. You aren't going to leave this time." He pushed back into Westin's touch, then put a hand over his mouth as if that could keep his wail from spilling out. "You aren't going to leave and I won't have to leave you. I'll rile you up but I'll keep you safe. You're mine. My one-and-only." He shivered violently. "Yes. Yes, West. Even though I'm trouble. You won't stop?"

"Come back up here," Westin ordered, distantly alarmed at how easy giving orders was becoming. But when he gently slid his fingers free, Sun came back up to be enfolded in his arms, and he was all warm skin and a sweet mouth at Westin's throat. A risk and a worry. Trouble, but also what let Westin shut his eyes and breathe. He might wish for a scent that better matched what Sun wanted, but the citrus-and-herb wasn't unpleasant. It was a scent for a steady, settled older man, because that was what Sun desired. "You *are* trouble," Westin agreed with him, nuzzling his hair and petting the freckles at his nape. "A wolfling and a brat." Another shiver went through Sun. Westin's blood stayed hot, but his thoughts were clear at last. "*My* brat," he ventured quietly, and slid his fingers back inside of Sun to elicit both a tortured cry and then a weak moan against his neck.

"Lark-in-my-hand," Westin realized aloud, and gave Sun another kiss amid the sound of heavy rain and quiet, distant, Solace House conversation.

Epilogue

The sun was shining and the air held the faint scent of flowers and wet earth. Spring was a lovely time to begin negotiations. Granted, Westin had started negotiations on much worse days, in much worse conditions, so he was inclined to favor the crisp air and even the slight chill that came with it. Nonetheless, he took it as a blessing from the fae that though he was in a large room filled with people he'd rather avoid, that room had many windows that overlooked one of the palace gardens, and the garden was in full bloom.

From his seat at the vast, round table, Westin could only see the tops of the garden walls, overgrown with small pink roses and a patch of moss on the shadowed side, and the branch of a tree heavy with white blossoms, but he'd rather that view than look at the wealthy, prideful nobles and their guards, all gathered about and looking for gossip instead of taking their seats at the table.

Perhaps they were waiting for the king to sit. If so, the king seemed content to make them wait. But Westin didn't look in that direction yet either. Maybe Westin should have also waited, but this was not, officially, a formal gathering, and he still wasn't certain he even wanted to be here, so he didn't move. It was just possible that he'd been invited to this meeting, this start of negotiations, out of politeness, or that the new king was going to take charge and Westin was little more than a figurehead.

Or scapegoat, should things go wrong. But that was a risk with any negotiation, and Westin had headed so many now over the years that he hoped his reputation would speak for him. Anyway, the new king wasn't really new, and if Westin considered the entirety of the past twenty-five years and beyond, then this king had been king the whole time, if uncrowned.

He wondered if the other beat-of-fours here realized that. Some of them were young; they might not know that the one they called the Traitor King had been the intended ruler all along. Of course, some of those here were young because the older generations had been killed or weakened by twenty years of in-fighting that the so-called traitor had finally put an end to.

That was the danger of time passing. People forgot what once was, even with the Great Library at their disposal.

Westin had requested information from the library when he had first received the invitation to be here. Yet he felt wildly unprepared now, sitting alone—almost alone—among finery and youthful faces. Some of these nobles could likely barely remember the time before the warring. Some might not have known it at all. Some didn't know him. Their occasional glances toward him were likely curiosity about the gray-haired, somewhat simply dressed man among them.

Westin didn't look back at them. He considered their sworn guards—each noble was permitted two unarmed sworn guards when within the palace, but for this meeting, because of the size of the room, or as a precaution, each noble was only allowed one. A few had no guard to accompany them, perhaps they considered themselves to be warrior enough, but most did have guards, silent and watchful.

But the sworn guards in the room were outnumbered by the palace guards at every corner and by the door and several of the windows. In addition, the king's husband—first husband—was ever armed and armored. As was the king. Even here, at the start of negotiations over the fuss around a wedding.

Twenty years of fighting. Twenty-five years of suspicion and fear. Then the incident that winter. Westin could not blame anyone for their fears or their precautions. But it did indicate these meetings would be tense, to say the least.

He considered the garden again and the tree with all the white flowers. The scent from the blossoms must have been delicate, because the perfumes around him continued to wash it away.

A jarring mix of scents, in all honesty. Westin was again grateful for the windows and the size of the room. It meant tetchy beat-of-fours could keep space between them and that the many windows prevented all their expensive perfumes from becoming too overwhelming to someone sensitive to those things. The sunlight would help him avoid headaches if Westin had to examine tiny handwriting on any ancient documents. His eyes were not what they used to be, and even the investment in magnifying glass lenses, fitted to wire frames that looped over his ears for stability, did not quite make up for the lost clarity of youth.

With that in mind, he pulled his lenses from a pocket of his robe and slipped them into place so he wouldn't end up squinting later.

From beside him, above his shoulder, came a mournful sigh.

Westin ignored it for the moment to pat his robe back into place. His finest, which of course was nowhere near as fine as the robes on the proud peacocks and preening robins gathered in this room, but was hardly shabby. He'd chosen it as a matter of pride but also to keep some of the creeping chill at bay—another hazard of age, even for those who didn't have bad memories of cold nights.

He reached up to check his long braid, painstakingly bedecked with glass beads and tiny strips of gold wire only that morning, but Sun batted his hand away.

"Don't touch it." Sun was firm. "You look incredible and that's all you need to worry about."

That was hardly all, but Westin glanced up.

Standing beside Westin's chair, Sun met his eyes, made a little punched-out noise, then turned his attention back to the rest of the room.

"Not the lenses too," he complained, breathless but snotty about it. He was ridiculous about what he thought of Westin's looks even now with silver cuffs all down the shells of his ears to match the threads of silver in his hair. His lips were pushed out in a slight pout, even while he kept watch on the various nobles milling around. "Your hair done as a proper beat-of-four and the lenses that make you look yet more serious than you already are? And I must behave? You will owe me when this is over."

"Oh?" Westin asked with mild interest, playing along because dealing with his husband was more entertaining than trying to suss out which people in this room were going to be a problem. Negotiations were easier if his mind was open to everyone at the start, he'd found, and he would need to be especially sharp here. Soothing noble pride and noble tempers with regard to a wedding should not have been worse than stepping in to try to keep peace during decades of warring. But since one was the conclusion of the other—hopefully—Westin was possibly right to worry.

It wasn't going to be easy in any case. Westin's skills as an arbiter had been called upon often in the last twenty years, but even he had never dealt with this many noble families at the same time, all of them vying for attention and victory.

"What is it you think I owe you?" Westin asked to keep himself from examining the others in the room one by one, though he would be doing that soon enough anyway.

Sun hummed. He put a hand on Westin's shoulder and bent down to whisper.

"Your mouth." His lips brushed Westin's ear. "In that garden out there. It's a familiar-looking garden."

Westin doubted his knees would enjoy kneeling on a stone path or moss-covered ground. Nonetheless, he considered it.

"With the lenses on, then?" he wondered. Sun had been obsessed with them from the moment Westin had reluctantly agreed he needed them. Westin had thought it another sign of age that might make him undesirable, but much like the mostly gray color of his hair or the crinkles at the corner of his eyes, Sun liked them.

Sun liked them a lot.

He made the punched-out sound again and curled his fingers over Westin's shoulder. "Must you make eyes at everyone? They're staring at you."

"They are staring at *you*, brat." Westin looked up to observe Sun glaring at nearly everyone in the room and put his hand over Sun's to bring Sun's attention back to him. "Rather surprised you aren't trying to charm them."

Sun scoffed. "What for? They're all going to be focused on the king and maybe the new husband-to-be. *To-be*." Sun scoffed again. "I'd bet a whole season's beet crop that the king and his husband have made vows to the little one already. Doesn't matter what spectacle they want or what The Arlylian says. It's done."

Westin glanced over to one of the windows, where two large figures stood behind a smaller, slighter figure peering down at two books he had open and resting on a window ledge. The small one was almost completely hidden from the rest of the room by the larger men, which Westin assumed was intentional. He glanced over the room again, at the nobles in their best surreptitiously watching the trio at the window, at the guards, palace and personal, at the one pretty-but-scowling figure in the corner dressed like a well-paid library assistant but probably a Master Keeper. They all seemed to be younger now too.

He finally returned his attention to the three everyone else was staring at. The larger two were talking to each other, not aloud, but in glances and looks, with an occasional shrug, like a pair who had known each other for most of their lives, but also like outguards in hostile territory who didn't want to risk their words being overheard.

Westin considered the largest man first. Mil Wulfa, he of the stories and songs. A legitimate hero, by most accounts. About forty or so, Westin thought, and wondered idly if Mil Wulfa would have left the Outguard on his own if circumstances had not led him to where he was now. But the Wulfa family had long been palace guards, and if this one had run off with a Canamorra at a young age, he had to have known what he was marrying into.

He probably didn't like or want any of this fuss, but was smart enough to know it was necessary. Twenty years of warring couldn't end without something to mark it or to give people hope. Nor could all the feuds and enmities that had built up between the noble houses during those years of war fade away without some concessions to the pride and honor of every family in this room. This wedding spectacle was necessary, but it was also a logistical and practical nightmare, particularly in matters of security.

Especially when one was marrying a sparkling little librarian. Every single person in this room, and probably in the palace and capital beyond, knew the librarian was a weakness. Oh, he was of a beat-of-four family with no scandal or feuds attached to it, and he would make a far better diplomat than the king's first husband. This alliance would strengthen the king's rule in countless ways. But he was a weakness too, vulnerable and hardly a fighter. Young and, judging from what Westin had so far observed, prone to getting lost in books. If anyone wanted leverage over the king—and everyone did—they were going to go after the librarian.

Westin moved his attention to Mil Wulfa's hand, on his librarian's shoulder much like Sun's hand on *his* shoulder. A loving, caring gesture. But even that revealed fear.

Together with his husband, Mil and the king had formed a wall around their prize. That revealed fear too. But also a promise to any noble thinking to come for the little one.

Westin nodded. "Oh, yes, they're already married." He paused, thoughtful but pointed. "Little?" The librarian wasn't that much shorter than Sun.

"Little," Sun repeated himself, ridiculously sulky for a man glaring at every noble and sworn guard in the room. "You think he's pretty."

"He *is* pretty." Westin kept hold of Sun's hand. "Soft, though, as you accuse me of being. Delicate. He's probably hardly any trouble at all." Westin considered the known attempt on the librarian's life and all the rumors about how the king and his husband had struggled to woo him that had reached Solace House and therefore reached Westin in the heart of Corilyeth territory. He amended his words. "At least, not your kind of trouble." He watched Mattin of the Arlylian turn and look up with wide, wide eyes, as if perhaps just noticing that his husbands flanked him. Sunlight glinted off the many sparkles in his hair. It gave Westin ideas. "You know, I will be honored well if I succeed here. We might ask the librarian where he gets his clasps and jewelry."

"For me?" Sun assumed immediately, smugness in his voice. "Only if there is enough honor left over that I might also find a new gold piece for you."

Westin stifled the urge to tell him it was nonsense, that he was too old to be draped in bits of gold. It would only make Sun more determined, and then Westin would have to hear, again, about the piercings the Rossick were alleged to do and narrowly avoid Sun trying to keep Westin's cock in gold chains permanently so that everyone would know who it belonged to.

Westin shifted in place nonetheless, also far too old to feel a spark at the thought and yet the spark existed and warmed him through.

It would likely only hurt the once, he reasoned. Although, he did wonder who Sun imagined was going to see his cock outside of the occasional visit to a public bath when traveling. Sun would see it. That was what mattered.

"You know I don't need gold," Westin finally said, as he always said, and glanced up in time to catch Sun's sneer.

"Half the people in this room are eyeing you, no matter that you're old enough to be their father."

Grandfather, for some of them. Westin kept that to himself too, as well as his exasperated sigh. "I don't think the country sees me as you see me, lark."

"You're so smart and yet so silly." Sun tossed his head. "There are Rossick here, you know," he added, a sly fox.

Westin took a breath to steady himself. But, "Are you testing me, brat? You already know it's yours. *I* am yours. Go find a Rossick now, if you're willing to let one touch my cock."

Sun harrumphed, sounding more like a man of Westin's age than his own.

"I mean it," Westin added, quieter. "If you want it, it's yours. That remains my promise to you."

"Fuck off," Sun said, equally quiet. "It will be gorgeous. You're gorgeous, Wes. It's annoying."

"I am in my sixth decade," Westin reminded him. "I'm old enough to be your father too, if I had been a more reckless youth."

"Your mouth," Sun answered decidedly. "Although it's been a while since you've bent me over something." His pout was audible. "Neglecting me. Leaving me empty. Have you decided you prefer librarians?"

Westin didn't know why that made him smile. "If I fuck you in a garden in daylight, they might kick us out of the palace."

"Then we could go back home. Away from these people. This place." All at once, Sun was serious. "Everyone here is a threat."

"I know, lark. I know."

Westin let his gaze drift to the second large figure by the window and the biggest threat in the room. Arden of the Canamorra wore only one tiny bit of jewelry for the moment: a simple golden cuff on one ear. He had not bothered with a crown, either from habit and temperament or because these negotiations were supposed to be about a wedding and he wanted to be thought of as a mere betrothed.

He was a handsome man, not as obvious about it as his first husband, who had Sun's ability to stun with a glance. Arden drew attention in a different way, and Westin didn't think it had anything to do with a throne or a crown, although that certainly helped in this room. Maybe it was the scar down the side of his face, but Westin suspected it was that Arden *had* to be watched, for he was observant, careful, and clever. A seemingly unremarkable outguard who had killed a king.

And he was Canamorra. The name itself was a terror to many, a legend to most. Westin couldn't imagine growing up with that name when he could barely handle his own. Arden intimidated the other nobles in the room without trying although Westin also suspected that Arden could and would do it on purpose if he felt like it or felt he needed to.

He was a killer, Westin decided, but unlike sworn guards or outguards. It was difficult to say if that was a result of his childhood or an innate quality of the Canamorra. At least, until Westin turned his head and caught a glimpse of the king's sister, Jola of the Canamorra, seated and chatting with Cael of the Rossick, both of them also observant, careful, and clever.

Westin turned back to the king, who was stroking the side of his librarian's face and looking savagely pleased at the pink flush that followed.

Mil Wulfa seemed to enjoy it as well, though he still kept one hand near his sword.

Two killers. But they wanted peace as they wanted their flower of a librarian, and Westin had no doubt they would do whatever it took to achieve each.

Though if it came to a choice between one or the other, they would choose their flower. Westin had no doubt of that and could not argue with it. After all, he had been prepared to walk out of these negotiations at the mere suggestion of Sun wanting his cock. Peace was important, but so were husbands.

Having internally settled on the true state of things, Westin sighed. "If the nobles here are smart, they will flatter that little Arlylian and give him whatever he wants but not threaten him in any way."

Sun shifted slightly, putting a hand to his belt and not his sword hilt since sworn guards were not supposed to be armed. Sun undoubtedly still was, but at least not with a sword.

"Since when are nobles smart?" He didn't say it quietly, but most beat-of-fours ignored sworn guards that weren't their own and Westin hoped the nobles around them would continue pretending to ignore Sun no matter how handsome he was with silver in his hair. "If they were smart, we wouldn't be here. If they were smart, we wouldn't have had to struggle to keep Corilyeth lands out of danger for twenty fucking years."

Across the room, the king turned. His eyes met Westin's.

Westin didn't look away, although he tightened his hold on his hissing ferret. "Do you blame the Canamorra for that, or everyone else?"

"Any of them. All of them." Sun might have been looking at Arden too. "Everyone who thought it was their right then because they probably *still* think it's their right."

Westin stroked his thumb across the back of Sun's hand to quiet his growling. "They'll be smart now or pay the price."

Several of the well-dressed bodies near Westin stepped aside or turned to look at him.

Arden's mouth moved in a hint of a smile, but probably not for having overheard Westin. He continued teasing the smaller of his husbands for the amusement or arousal of the larger of his husbands.

Westin tore his attention away to look up at *his* husband, ignoring the shocked though very fashionable Balylithan who was regarding Sun with either horror or irritated desire. Possibly both. He tried to lighten his tone. "Are you worried?"

Sun gave him a look. "You're worried, so I am worried. How did they even hear of you anyway? There are no songs about *you* leaving your noble family to join the Outguard." He grumbled that, as he had grumbled it since hearing the first song about young Arden. Stolen valor, he called it, as though Arden had written the songs himself.

"Probably from someone else in the guard," Westin guessed. "It doesn't matter."

"It does. It puts you smack in the middle of all this."

"Us," Westin corrected him, smiling for no logical reason.

Sun huffed. "*You* means me. You're mine. You know this, West."

"I do." Westin smiled a little wider, then pulled Sun's hand to his mouth so that he could kiss the inside of his wrist and enjoy the warmed-violet scent that never really left Sun now. "No amount of pouting beat-of-fours could ever rival you and the trouble you stir up."

"They'll try," Sun promised, veering close to a growl again. He lowered his voice and was frowning when he bent his head to speak. "If every single one of these noble families is to be appeased by being allowed to contribute to this shitshow, it will be chaos."

Westin nodded. Sun's opinions on such things were rarely wrong. Sun had been with him through each negotiation over the past decades, whether they were to protect the people on Corilyeth lands or to establish peace elsewhere, and he had always been good at determining what others wanted.

Sun lowered his voice even more. "If anyone is going to try again to take the throne, they will do it soon. Probably in the midst of all that chaos while the besotted king and his first consort are distracted."

Westin nodded again, slower. "I suspect the king and his husband are aware of this. I'd be very surprised if they weren't."

"But the nobles want a showy end to the fighting, and a showy new beginning, and their chance to push themselves into favor, so a large, public wedding it must be." Sun wrinkled his nose. "Our wedding was better."

"I don't think the people would like the idea of the king hand-fasting to an Arlylian in a curtained booth in Solace House." Westin was surprised his tone stayed mild, but then, the warmed-violet scent of Sun was nearly guaranteed to soothe him. "Though Solace House would love the business."

"You think you're funny," Sun complained. "Fuck you."

He got another horrified yet admiring glance from the Balylithan.

"Brat," Westin declared with fondness, perhaps drawing some eyes to him as well. But he kept his serious question for the two of them alone. "We can leave. I am not obligated to be here."

"And *not* know what's going on?" Sun was outraged. "Leaving it to these people to keep the peace?" His disdain was obvious. "They fuck it up and we've got another twenty years of struggling to look forward to."

"Ah." Westin kissed the inside of Sun's wrist again. "So you don't care about the particulars, only the results? I could send you out, give you some coin to go shopping so you won't be bored by all this."

"Fuck you," Sun said again, and without any concern for dignity—his or Westin's—squeezed around the table and plopped onto Westin's lap.

There was a stir throughout the room; many nobles might fuck a sworn guard but few married them. And the ones that did likely did not sit this way during important meetings. Westin focused on pulling Sun against his chest to try to force an impudent wolfling to be still, and enjoyed the silky texture of Sun's hair as he nuzzled it shamelessly. Sun had two knives Westin could feel: one beneath his shirt and vest, another in a sleeve.

"Bored?" Sun challenged. "You think I'll be bored? I won't be able to take my eyes off you." He dropped his voice to a whisper. "They'll come for you too, you know, if they think it will help. They always do when you do this, and the stakes are higher now."

So Sun was already prepared. There were probably more knives Westin hadn't yet found.

Westin raised his head, unsurprised to find many staring at them, including the three by the window. The little Arlylian had bright, curious eyes.

"The two of us," Westin whispered back, his gaze meeting the king's again, "against everyone in this room but those three." He hesitated before adding, "And those two." He carefully lifted his fingers to gesture toward Jola of the Canamorra and Cael of the Rossick. "And possibly that Master Keeper in the corner if librarians are as loyal to each other as outguards are." Sun wriggled, perhaps objecting, perhaps just wanting to feel Westin's cock twitch. "That's why he chose us, because we're former outguards, or perhaps because of the reputation the Corilyeth have earned these twenty years. Or perhaps because he knows he's not the first beat-of-four to marry an outguard and he is counting on us for help."

Sun abruptly settled. "You think he knows that?"

Westin spoke against Sun's ear and all the pretty cuffs Westin had personally put there that morning. "I think he knows that." The how didn't matter, at least not for the moment, although Westin almost glanced back to Jola and Cael and their quiet, intimate conversation. "I believe he wants peace, and he wants his Arlylian, but if it comes down to it... well. I understand what he might choose. His bear of a husband would choose the same. I'd count on that. But he prefers the first option. That's why I'm here. Oh." Westin considered that again. "That's exactly why I'm here. An outsider but a noble. An outguard in a pairing of love, with years of experience serving as judge to other beat-of-fours."

"He could have just said so," Sun nearly moaned it, definitely wriggling to try to get Westin hard, grinding his hips in front of every important beat-of-four in the country. Though admittedly, only a few of them seemed scandalized.

"Would *you* have?" Westin asked the back of Sun's head, nosing at the cuffed shell of one ear. "Would you even say such a thing to me now, wolfling?"

"The king is not a…" Sun stopped, thinking the idea through. "You think he's like me." His voice was impossible to read.

"If his life was even a fraction of what the songs about him say," Westin admitted. "Then yes, he is like you." Slow to trust and open to only a handful of people. "So what do you think? You were better at spotting what people want long before Hely improved your skills with lessons."

"*Hely*," Sun growled, but reflexively, because he knew it amused Westin and not for any other reason. He took a deep breath. "The three at the window are far outnumbered by the potential threats in this room. Even the nobles inclined to peace or to like the king all have their own agenda. Even you have an agenda, though it's only to protect what is yours. And that means he can never really trust. Maybe he never trusted anyone until he met them. His husbands." Sun stopped for a moment, giving away more than he liked to, but only to Westin, who was allowed to know. "And he is our hope for peace."

There was no denying that, unless one happened to be a foolishly ambitious noble.

"If he gets you killed, I'll kill him myself," Sun added, calm about it. "If I can get through that hulking brute of a first husband. I might be older and slower now, but the big ones always have a weakness. West," Sun stopped again, then continued on, lofty and light, "do you think they're all imagining you fucking me like this?"

Some of them undoubtedly were. Westin was too old and too trained by Sun to feel much embarrassment about it anymore.

"Yes." He kissed Sun's ear. At the window, the king smiled again. "So we're agreed then?"

Sun squirmed, once again intentionally. Thankfully, it took a little more to get Westin hard these days, so when Sun stood up and took his place back at Westin's shoulder, Westin wasn't too visibly aroused. The table was there to hide much in any case.

Sun scanned the room like the former outguard and survivor he was, then murmured, "Agreed. But you still owe me your mouth."

Westin captured Sun's hand again simply to hold it. He met the eyes of the king and slowly inclined his head. Arden's dark eyes filled with fire, then he began gently leading his husbands toward the table and the rest of the nobles in the room began to follow suit.

"It's a lovely day to begin such an endeavor," Westin remarked, reassured to hear Sun's scoff. Whatever Westin might have added, he forgot when a slight figure in a brightly embroidered robe dropped into the seat on his left and immediately leaned closer.

Mattin of the Arlylian, who almost definitely was not supposed to be so close to someone he didn't know, judging from the alarm on the faces of both his hovering husbands, was no more than twenty-six, with warm brown eyes full of interest and arms full of the two books he seemed to have forgotten that he held.

"Westin of the Corilyeth?" He named Westin without any hesitation over the abandoned fifth beat. "I'm so glad you came. Your reputation precedes you, and I knew you'd be helpful."

"Sass." Mil Wulfa's gruff, quiet objection was waved away.

Mattin finally put his books down, scooting them to one side as if he was aware that he was not in his proper seat and would have to move soon. Or *be* moved, likely. Mil Wulfa appeared more than capable of simply hefting him up and depositing him somewhere else.

"*You* invited me?" Westin couldn't help a moment of confusion, particularly when the king stood pointedly at Mattin's other shoulder like a worried mother hen.

"I've read so many reports of you." As if sensing danger, Mattin lifted an arm to gesture behind him. He clucked his tongue when the king captured his hand and did not return it. "As well as the finished documents of agreements you helped get made. Well, copies of those. I'm a Master Keeper. They go back to your time in the Outguard. You witnessed quite a few judgments and we—the others at the library and I—have long suspected you had a hand in those too. More than as a witness, I mean. So I wanted to thank you for coming. Will you visit the library if you have time while you're here, or perhaps when you return for the wedding? Several of the Keepers would love to get your memories of those events in the records."

"Dear heart," said the king, in a tone Westin didn't think he wanted to read. Westin hadn't been in the Great Library for over twenty years but he remembered what the assistants were like, although he doubted that was what the little Arlylian meant.

But Sun might have thought so. He slipped his hand free of Westin's in order to press down hard and unyielding on his shoulder.

"Finally, some appreciation." Sun was pleasant, almost charming, despite the fact that sworn guards generally didn't speak up in such moments. He also knew what library assistants were like. "I've been telling him he's special for nearly three decades now. But maybe he'll believe it from you."

Mattin got a worried look on his face but had no chance to ask any further questions. As predicted, he was picked up and set on his feet and then urged one chair down, where Mil Wulfa then stood at his elbow between him and the now-empty seat.

The seat the king sat in, putting Westin on his right.

"You trust me that much?" Westin heard himself asking, his surprise at being so honored undoubtedly obvious.

Arden of the Canamorra gave Westin a careful study. "The guard who left and took the infamous wolfling with him? Even if Mil and I hadn't known you for that, Mattin put together information on you for me to read." He lifted his chin to address Sun. "Does he always fret like this, Sunlark of South Burrow?"

Sun relaxed his grip, though only slightly. "Until he has resolved the problem, yes. Most people don't notice."

Westin got the feeling Arden noticed many things, and what he didn't, Mil did. And what *he* didn't, Mattin would discover in a dusty volume dragged from the depths of the Great Library.

An odd light filled Westin's chest, and a faint, sweet scent drifted to him for a moment. Perhaps it was the white blossoms. Perhaps it was the fae blessing of hope.

"This is indeed a problem that needs resolving if we want this peace to last." Arden was serious, nodding to someone sitting down at Westin's right. To Cael of the Rossick, calm and unimpressed. Arden suddenly smiled, looking almost like a boy. "I couldn't leave it all to Cael."

Westin inhaled to steady himself.

"Then I am happy to help. Although all I really do is listen." He ignored the noise of protest from Sun. "That's all most people want, really. To be heard."

Mattin had a pencil in his hand. Where he'd pulled it from, Westin didn't know, but he appeared to be writing down Westin's words.

"Excellent," Mattin muttered as he scribbled, leaving Westin to be studied once again by two husbands and a Rossick. Studied by the entire room, perhaps, with everyone no doubt wondering why someone from an obscure and fallen family had this much attention.

The first day of negotiations had not even begun and Westin found himself longing for tea, or at least some sort of distraction.

Sun, fae-blessed brat that he was, spoke in a carrying voice.

"Keeper Arlylian, those are some beautiful clasps in your hair. I don't suppose you know of a place in the capital that does work in gold? I'm looking for a particular piece."

Westin tugged Sun's wrist to his mouth. A king and two husbands and dozens of nobles were before him. *Peace* was before him, if he tried. He hoped the blossoms in view were there to tell him to try. To show him what was waiting for him if he succeeded.

Flowers that Sun liked, and a garden where he owed Sun the use of his mouth, and more lovely days like this one, even with the hint of a chill.

A sign, perhaps. Hope again.

Westin sighed and let go, turning his attention at last to the waiting nobles.

"Shall we begin?"

The End

Blessed

Introduction

THIS IS AN ALTERNATE universe version of an existing story, A Suitable Consort (For the King and His Husband), but can be (and has been) read on its own by people who have no idea about the original. I basically wrote it because some people were speculating on the original and the alpha-or-omeganess of the mains. So I thought about it too, lol. If you *have* read the original, know this mostly is the same, but the timeline is more drawn out. And obviously there is the change of the canon-compliant heats and the like.

This version is also the adult-rated version. The fade-to-black original version is available elsewhere for those interested.

Blessed – Part One

MATTIN DIDN'T LIKE TO think that he *stumbled* into the king's rooms, but the guards at the outer door moved toward him as if to catch him if he fell, so he certainly wasn't graceful. He ignored his blush and the heat beneath his skin that was fading too slowly for his liking. His cool bath that morning had not soothed any of his aches and pains, but had at least left him clean and smelling of icy mint, which he hoped would keep his mind clear enough for him to get some work done today.

He'd fallen behind, caught unawares once again by his lust-fever despite how it occurred regularly every four months in everyone fae-blessed. Anyone with fae blood was afflicted—given gifts—in some way, although some fortunate souls were granted little more than occasional discomfort and others experienced no discomfort or fevers of any kind but had drive enough to match the needs of the third kind. *Blessed*, the third kind were called, though Mattin had never felt so.

The lust-fevers, or heats, as he'd heard some refer to them recently, were a messy, sticky, uncomfortable, humiliating business, and that didn't even bring in the care required to not end up with child should Mattin ever be so fortunate as to have a partner, or how the heats interrupted his work.

Mattin loved his work. He enjoyed reading, and studying, and digging through records until he found information that was needed. It helped that books and scrolls didn't care if he was a bit on the plain side for a Blessed, and too insignificant, even for a beat-of-four, for anyone to take a real interest in. Not seriously anyway, not beyond conversation at parties.

Not that Mattin went to many parties these days. The palace was finally starting to feel settled and calm again after years of warring, coups, and chaos, but there was much work to be done to keep it that way, and Mattin was happier to be useful to the new king than he was to fuss over his appearance just to attend a party where he'd end up tipsy on wine in a corner ignored by all and far from the king and his husband on the other side of the room if they happened to be there.

Mattin enjoyed a chance to show off pretty clothes and any new jewelry purchases, but he'd made a special effort to look nice for *those* parties. It was expected, even though the king and his husband were not the sort to wear much jewelry—or care for parties, to be honest. But Mattin's extra effort had not resulted in much. He'd taken to bringing his work with him to the last few such gatherings he'd attended, and no one except for the king and his husband had interrupted him, which said it all.

Mattin did care. He was honest enough with himself to admit that. But his lack of appeal was only on his mind now because he was fresh, or not-so-fresh, from a fever, and stingingly aware that his lust-fevers wouldn't be so difficult or exhausting if he had help in getting through them. A friend would have done, if he found one he trusted enough to let them see him… like that.

He shuddered a little at the thought, nearly bumping into a chair as he made his way to the king's study—unoccupied by the king, as usual. Arden of the Canamorra was a noble with a noble's education, and had a sharp mind, but he had also spent almost two decades living the active life of an outguard with his guard husband, and sitting at a desk for any length of time was something he avoided when he could.

Of course, at this hour of the morning, Arden would not have been at his desk anyway. He and his husband were still in their sitting room enjoying breakfast. If they hadn't been, Mattin didn't think the guards would have waved him in.

Mattin paused on the other side of the thick curtains that separated the study from the sitting room, straightening his clothes and inhaling the cooling scent of mint to keep all lingering fever thoughts at a distance. Then, with one anxious tug on his long braid, he pushed the curtain aside.

The conversation from the two at the table before the fireplace stopped.

Arden—that was, the king, as Mattin kept forgetting to call him of late—rose to his feet, entirely too much concern on his handsome, scarred face as he towered over Mattin.

Mattin quickly looked away from Arden to Arden's husband, only to find Mil outright scowling.

"You look ready to fall over," Mil growled, not pleased. "Are you ill? It's those useless clothes you wear, Sass." He insisted upon the nickname and Mattin was too flustered and tired to offer his usual polite objection. "They may be pretty and fine, and they suit you well, but we've had weeks of rain and now snow and yet you never dress for it."

"My love," Arden remarked to cut Mil off, "be gentle with him. He seems ready to fall over as it is."

"I..." It was all Mattin managed. Then Mil was up, towering over Mattin even more than his husband did, and Mattin was being carefully but firmly urged onto the cushioned sofa on one side of their table and Arden was sitting back down to offer Mattin tea in Mattin's favorite cup.

Mattin should not have a favorite cup at the king's table and had certainly never been so improper as to say he did. Nonetheless, the cup, painted with delicate nasturtium vines, seemed to be on their table every morning now. At least, every morning that Mattin came here to share information with Arden at Arden's request and to help him and Mil plan their days.

That was a task not required or expected of a Master Keeper at the Great Library, but Mattin was happy to do it, and the palace's Head of House, Cael of the Rossick, was grateful for the help in corralling "their stubborn king and his only slightly more reasonable husband." A funny description, as most nobles in the palace thought Mil was the uncouth, stubborn one and Arden—noble, even if also Canamorra—the one capable of being reasoned with.

Mattin had to hold his cup in both hands to keep his tremors from causing a splash, but he didn't miss how Arden and Mil exchanged a glance at that.

"I'm getting a healer," Mil announced when their look ended, and started to stand up again.

"No, no!" Mattin rushed to assure him, taking one hand from his teacup and immediately spilling some tea onto the plate that had mysteriously appeared on the table in front of him. The tea soaked into a sweet bun. Mattin stared at the bun blearily for a moment, certain he'd heard the king say that he didn't care for sweet buns with raisins and that Mil preferred the buns with cream in the center. Yet there was a sweet bun with raisins and honey, what Mattin liked, and it had company on the plate.

"Yes, I think," Arden calmly overruled Mattin, then reached over to take Mattin's cup and fill it with more tea before handing it back. "You're unwell, Mat—Keeper Arlylian. Drink that now."

Arden said it pleasantly, but it was an order.

Mattin started to grow hotter in a way that had nothing to do with blushes or his proximity to the fireplace. Lust-fevers were slow to fade sometimes, and harder to manage when he was around Arden and Mil, who were fae-touched in the opposite way as Mattin and were unfortunately also large and handsome and smelled wonderful as only those fae-gifted could smell. Mattin couldn't even explain it to himself, but they did.

They smelled like a good nest should smell.

It was dreadfully embarrassing although Mattin tried not to be obvious about sniffing them.

"I'm not unwell," he muttered at last, looking away from Arden's dark eyes as he drank his tea. The cup was plucked from his trembling hands the moment he was finished and filled again, with more milk added. Mil leaned across the table to nudge the plate closer to Mattin.

Mattin kept his attention on the tea, hoping the steam would explain away any red in his cheeks as the king and his husband unknowingly acted like a pair of Gifted out to court a Blessed, offering food and care and the Blessed's favorite things.

He sipped from the second cup, swallowed, then murmured, "Thank you. But I'm not unwell."

"I must disagree." Arden continued to sound mild but Mattin wasn't fooled. Arden was crafty, as many a beat-of-four in the palace had learned too late.

"First, you disappear for three days," Mil remarked, "then you show up looking like the fae brought you back from death."

That wasn't an idle comparison. Mattin raised his head without thinking and found Mil glaring at him and Arden together. Arden had quite famously been brought back to life by the fae after dying in Mil's arms. Mattin turned toward him too, then away when Arden reached out to stroke his husband's cheek with the back of one hand.

"I am sorry, my love," he said, as he always said whenever that day was mentioned. Since it was part of how Arden had ended up on the throne, it was mentioned frequently.

"Be that as it may," Mil continued grumpily after a few moments of silence that left Mattin dizzy, "there's still something wrong with our Sass."

It tricked Mattin into looking up again. He did his best to focus. "There isn't," he insisted. "Anyway, we have more important matters to discuss. I'm sorry I was absent, but I have the information you requested on the old Savirin lands."

"Now that I think on it," Arden commented in a suddenly breezy tone, "I seem to recall you being absent like this once before, Keeper Arlylian. At least once. When you first started to come to council meetings." He took a bun from the plate before Mattin, tore it in two, and held one of the halves out to Mattin until Mattin took it.

The bun smelled amazing. Mattin's stomach gurgled loudly enough to probably be heard by the distant guards and he ducked his head to try to eat with some decorum instead of shoving the whole thing in his mouth.

The rest of the bun was placed in his hand before he'd finished chewing. He looked up. Arden gazed back at him. The light in his eyes might have been fondness or it might have been playful teasing about Mattin's appetite that Arden held in. "There's more," Arden told him, voice a little rough, "help yourself."

Mattin glanced to Mil, who had a similar light in his eyes. For that reason, despite his gnawing hunger, Mattin took his time breaking the bun into smaller pieces to finish it, eating each one as neatly and carefully as possible. Then he went back to his tea. He wasn't about to get teased for eating like a beast in front of them. They wouldn't care; they were used to life outside the palace and the rough work of outguards, but they knew Mattin thought differently about such matters.

Soft hands, Mil also liked to call him. Or *sparkly wee thing*. The kind of person to use a daintily painted teacup and not the sturdy mugs they used.

"I know how to feed myself." Mattin said it firmly.

"You sure about that?" Mil squinted at him. "Are you thinner than usual too? Fuck me, I know he's a Master Keeper at the Great Library, but a keeper of his own is what he needs. Someone to take a stand when he works all night and falls asleep in his chair or forgets his cloak for the dozenth time."

Arden handed Mattin another bun from Mattin's own plate. Well, from the plate of buns they had given him.

"You could eat your own breakfasts, instead of nitpicking mine," Mattin grumbled at them, then jolted. "That wasn't sass," he added quickly. "It wasn't."

Mil grinned widely. "Feeling better already to be sassing his king like that."

Mattin slouched down in his chair to tear his bun apart. Even with that, he managed to finish it in record time.

"A third?" Arden asked smoothly. "Or perhaps some fruit first?"

"How do you even have those buns here anyway?" Mattin wondered, *not* with sass, while accepting the orange slice Arden put into his palm. He hadn't even seen Arden peel the orange but he could smell it in the air, the citrus new and sharp among the warm tea and the honey on the buns. Beneath that, he could still smell Arden and Mil, their scents *hot* in that way that Gifted scents were, strong and only stronger when Mattin was weakened. The cool mint seemed entirely gone.

"Asked for 'em," Mil said around his slice of orange, which Arden continued to hand to each of them without taking any for himself. "You feeling better? You sure?"

"He doesn't want us to fuss, my love," Arden told his husband, sounding so deeply *saddened* by this that even though Mattin knew that Arden was doing it to get a response from him, he looked up with his protest ready.

His protest fell to nothing. They were both watching him expectantly, maybe even hopefully. It was a trick meant to tease the truth from him because they were nosy and Arden was commanding, but also because, for whatever reason, they cared.

Mattin shivered. He *had* forgotten his cloak today, but in his defense, he wasn't chilled. He wouldn't feel the cold again until at least tomorrow.

If he explained that, Mil would argue that Mattin's body was still affected by the cold even if Mattin didn't want to admit it, and he'd do better to be bundled up. Then Arden would gently chide Mil for scolding him before saying something about winter illnesses and how easily they spread, and Mattin would end up going back to his room for a cloak despite how it would take time from his schedule.

It wasn't because Mattin was a Blessed and they were Gifted, though many might think so, assuming that just because a Blessed might demand to be taken care of in bed, they wanted that the rest of the time too. It was simply that it was nice to have anyone care about Mattin here in the capital, far from home and his family. Mattin was, after all, the youngest of a youngest, and except for within the Great Library's walls, he was not especially noticeable or interesting. Unlike his king and his king's beloved husband.

They were both so incredible, Mattin reflected with a sadness of his own. Remarkable for leaving the palace behind when they had been younger than Mattin was now, and returning only out of duty. Heroes, the two of them. They had saved the palace and everyone in it from the last tyrannical and murderous ruler, with one of them dying in the attempt and the other acting so bravely songs had been written about it. Then they'd chosen to stay here to govern despite Arden's fear of acting cruelly like so many in his family had when they had ruled—the Canamorra were a family ancient, proud, and often terrible. Since then, he and Mil had worked hard to keep the peace, which only made them more heroic, at least to Mattin. And then, of course, both of them were fatally attractive in different ways: Mil, big and broad and seemingly rough. Arden, dark and watchful and only slightly smaller than his husband.

And Gifted, when many whispered that the fae-gifted were meant to serve the fae-blessed. It wasn't fair.

Mattin wouldn't have allowed himself to dwell on it if he'd been feeling better.

He sighed tiredly and ignored how alarmed they both grew at the sound.

"If you two weren't so... *you*, you'd recognize that I'm not ill. I'm just post-fever," he said to the refilled cup of tea set in front of him. "That's all. I'm Blessed. Didn't you know?" He'd always assumed others could smell it the way he could smell them. Most Gifted certainly seemed to have no trouble finding a Blessed if they wanted one, and those in between did as they pleased.

Silence fell and stayed. Mattin considered running but wasn't sure his legs would carry him.

Finally, Mil grunted. "Never seen anyone post-fever look like you did when you walked in."

"Blessed?" Arden asked, tone suspiciously light. "But Cael was surprised along with us when you were absent before. She was *worried*."

Cael of the Rossick, intimidating both for her family name and for her stern competence, had worried for Mattin. Mattin was going to die of embarrassment.

Arden carried on as if he didn't see Mattin's panic, although of course he did. "I know that though the timing differs for each of you Blessed, your fevers are every four months as long as you are of age and not with child. Which..." Arden's tone slipped into something darker. "Which I do not believe you are."

Mil made an unhappy sound. "Never heard a word of him with anyone, but I reckon mistakes can happen, even with friends and fever-partners."

"I'm not—" Mattin glared across the table at Mil, caught himself glaring, then sank back down to drink some of his third cup of tea. "I'm not pregnant," he hissed at last, horrified at the very idea though humiliatingly damp in his trousers to imagine getting that way. It didn't help that when he thought of a fever-breeding, he thought of Mil and Arden between his legs.

He was more than damp now and shuddered violently before trying to hide behind his teacup. "And I don't have a fever-partner or anyone else. *Obviously.*" He scrubbed one stinging cheek.

Arden reached for him without touching him. "Apologies, Keeper Arlylian. Truly. We were only concerned."

Mattin released another weary sigh and put the cup down. "I know."

He decided not to think about the look they exchanged then.

"So… there's no one?" Mil pressed after a pause, sitting back when Arden narrowed his eyes at him. "I mean," Mil turned to Mattin with innocence, real or false, "it's just that I thought it was easier for you to have someone with you for it. That's what they always said when they asked us to—"

He stopped far too abruptly.

Mattin felt a spike of something, not pain, not pleasure, not even envy. *Something*.

"You've helped Blesseds through their fevers before?" His voice held something unknown as well, which would never have happened if he'd been properly taken care of, or at least had remembered his fever coming and overfed himself in the days before it hit to make up for the toll it took on his body.

"Well, they asked." Mil glanced to his husband. "He's upset. I've upset him." It was clearly a demand for Arden to do something about it, as though Mil was sometimes like a fae-blessed with his husband and expected to be taken care of.

Arden looked at Mattin. "It was our pleasure to help. Although we haven't done so in some time. Not since before we ever returned to the palace. Mostly when we were younger. But it was an honor to do it." He said it seriously, the way people were supposed to have said it in ancient, and probably still embarrassing, rituals. "And a joy."

Mattin only barely kept himself from squirming in his seat. He was too close to his fever to handle learning this. He opened his mouth, then closed it with a snap and sat there until his stomach gurgled again.

"Shall I order food for you?" Arden suggested, almost tentative. *Almost*, but not quite, because he was Arden Canamorra. "A solid meal perhaps? The buns are not enough? You're still pale, Mattin—Master Arlylian."

"Did you do this for them too?" Mattin heard himself demand, and then, horrified with himself, jumped to his feet, nearly knocking into the table. "I'm sorry. I shouldn't have come here today. Usually, I stay in my office so that I can work without seeing anyone and…." He shut his mouth again when Mil growled.

"You *work* after your fevers? You're supposed to rest." Mil was still growling. It was making Mattin weak in entirely new ways. "Someone should make you rest if you won't, you wee, stubborn thing."

Someone meant Arden, and Mattin got a little more wet at the idea of Arden commanding him to stay in bed, no matter how politely Arden would phrase it.

"I can return tomorrow. I'll be better," Mattin promised quickly. Then his chin came up as the rest of Mil's words sank in. "Stubborn? I'm not... I'm not stubborn. You have to do this all on your own when you're like me. You wouldn't understand. But I'm fine. I just forget, sometimes. I'm working and I don't think to feed myself more in the days beforehand. Then I come out of it and I'm," weakened and exhausted, "more tired than I should be."

"*Like you*?" Mil asked, echoing him in confusion.

Arden was gentler. "I thought there were signs to warn you. I thought there were cravings, and temperature changes, and slowly increasing desires. You get absorbed in your work, Mattin—Keeper Arlylian, but to the point of that?"

"There's no one?" Mil asked again. "I don't understand."

"You wouldn't." Mattin crossed his arms over his chest. "It's a Blessed problem." Albeit one other Blesseds didn't seem to have. "It doesn't matter, really, except that I'm sorry I fell behind and failed you."

Arden's response was immediate. "You didn't."

"Sass," Mil began. He was probably going to apologize for not realizing the extent of Mattin's plainness.

"Really," Mattin cut him off firmly, "it's fine. Or it will be once I eat some more."

"And rest properly?" Arden wondered, mild again, worryingly so.

Arden Canamorra grew up with palace intrigue and bloody reprisals and the deaths of most his family. He didn't share his softer emotions with others often. Almost never, Mattin sometimes thought. And when he did, even sometimes when he was in the privacy of his sitting room with just his husband and Mattin, he'd hide them.

He did that now, because he was worried. For Mattin.

A long, soft whine escaped Mattin, silencing whatever Mil had been going to say and making Arden pull in a breath.

A weak, hungry, *unsatisfied* Blessed. That's what Mattin sounded like.

He looked into their suddenly fixed, intent gazes, one after the other, then was ashamed to say he squeaked before bolting from the room.

He bolted past the study in the same manner and then out of the door, leaving the guards to stare after him. His legs carried him to his room before they gave out, and he curled up on the soiled sheets he hadn't had a chance to send to be laundered while he tried to contemplate everything *but* the king or the king's husband's concern.

At least, until a knock on his door announced the arrival of food, specially ordered from the kitchens for him by the king and his husband.

Mattin waited a day in his room, as he should have done from the start, and then took a few days to keep to the library and make sure his contact with the king and his husband was limited to notes, which Mattin sent to Cael and had her pass them on.

When Mattin entered the council chamber after that, freshly bathed, his stylishly long hair held neatly in place with new clasps of colored glass in the shape of cherries, his stomach full of a meal that hadn't only been cold tea and stale pastries found in his office, he nodded in greeting to both the king and his husband and then kept to the back of the room as he always did.

When he saw them in their sitting room the following morning, Mattin's humiliating post-fever behavior was not spoken of. He spotted a sweet bun on the table, but it was not placed on a plate and set in front of him. His favorite teacup remained, but he poured his own tea into it.

He was warmed with gratitude at their thoughtfulness and saddened to know he would never be accidentally cared for again now that they knew about him. Foolish, to feel both things, but at least they were feelings Mattin could keep to himself.

Of course, it helped that he was far out of his fever time and that he had plenty of work to keep him distracted.

Some of the old families, the noblest of noble blood, of lines so ancient their names often held four beats, were still making trouble for Arden and the country's tentative peace. Their pride could not be allowed to cause more blood to be spilled, especially not Arden's. Mattin would not allow it, although admittedly, unlike Mil and Arden he was no warrior, and the best he could do was providing Arden with whatever information he required to appease or silence the more annoying beat-of-fours.

There was nothing more satisfying than watching Arden do just that. Well, perhaps some things were more satisfying but Mattin was unlikely to find out for himself. It was only unfortunate that Mattin had the regular work of a Master Keeper at the Great Library to keep him busy as well. Perhaps overly busy, at times.

Mattin didn't mean to fall asleep at his desk, as he had assured Mil more than once. He never intended to forget meals. There was just always something else that needed to be done and he got distracted.

The matter of cloaks... that was more that Mattin had other things on his mind. But it didn't matter much anyway. Mattin spent most of his time inside the library, and the spring and summer months meant he didn't need a cloak.

Mattin was sweating in his tiny office already and it was not even noon. He looked to his fireplace more than once, surprised each time to see no fire lit. He pulled at his clothes, newly made and surely not too tight around the collar despite how they tugged and pinched him today. He scowled at the ancient scroll in front of him, written in archaic language in faded ink, which was why the words melded together and were giving him a headache.

He would open the office's small window but the last time he'd tried, he'd unfortunately happened to hear a library assistant and member of the outguard fucking in some alcove behind the building. That happened from time to time. It was a game to the assistants, Mattin suspected, although he'd never been propositioned by any outguards when he'd been an assistant. He had spoken to outguards in the course of his duties, of course, but nothing had ever come of it. The palace had been different then, full of danger and spies and paranoia. Everyone had been tense and afraid, and Mattin wasn't the kind of person who could easily coax smiles from others. He shouldn't ache over it now. He shouldn't even be thinking of it, or how it would feel to have an outguard's callused hands tear away his fine, new clothes.

He wouldn't like that anyway, he was certain. Mattin was fond of his clothing and didn't want it torn, especially not for some one-off encounter with a guard, no matter how big or kind or Gifted they were.

But think of it he did, and the breathless sounds the assistant had been making, and realized he was growing aroused right as someone knocked quickly on the door. Thankfully, Mattin was seated at his desk and all anyone would see that might give him away was his reddened face.

Elbi, an assistant, gave him a small, almost nervous smile. "Apologies," she began before stepping into the room, which put her at Mattin's desk because Mattin's office truly was tiny. "We found these outside," she added in a strange tone, not meeting his eyes as she held up a pair of gloves, "and thought they might be yours or that you might know whose they were. They're very fine."

That they were, although they were obviously not Mattin's. The gloves were large, made of sturdy leather, and well used. They looked more like a guard's gloves than a librarian's, although they were also clearly well-made and would have cost more than most guards would spend. Most librarians too; Mattin was unusual for being noble and choosing to work here. That and his interest in fashions made him a good person to ask about the gloves, although he didn't know why Elbi seemed to expect him to hold onto them. She left the gloves on his desk and then ducked out of the room before Mattin could say a word. She shut the door behind her.

Mattin picked up the gloves to better examine them, so hot he was prickling with sweat and didn't want to imagine wearing anything so heavy. Just the weight in his palm was enough to make his cheeks sting, and the scent.... He knew the scent of the leather, anyone would, but this was something else on top of that. Something familiar. Something hot and strong.

He pulled the gloves away from his face when he realized he was sniffing them and hastily set them down so he could continue his work.

The words did not stop swimming. The room was sweltering. Mattin couldn't wait for summer to end and it had not even begun yet. His clothes *were* too tight, which was vexing. The gloves were heavy in his hands and warm against his face, their scent pleasing. He thought there was a hint of herbs beneath everything else, the kind that reminded him of remedies from a healer, as though the wearer had been bruised and worn ointment on their skin. The rest of the scent was confusing but good, weighty like the gloves themselves.

Mattin put them down. He picked them up. They were Mil's, he suspected, or maybe Arden's, or maybe shared between them. They shouldn't have been in the library unless Arden and Mil had stopped in. Although that meant they had been near and hadn't come to see Mattin.

Which was ridiculous. They had no reason to.

Mattin took a deep breath. He smelled *Gifted*. He felt Arden and Mil in his lungs and then in his blood, and licked sweat from his lip only to get the taste of leather instead.

He was so hot.

He was...

"Oh no," Mattin said aloud, and stumbled from his chair to the door. He had sense enough to stop Elbi and tell her he was leaving and why, and to ask if she wouldn't mind having something to eat sent to his room. Then he didn't remember much of anything, not clearly anyway, which he was pathetically grateful for when he woke in a moment of lucidity on the floor by the side of his bed with his face buried in the palm of one glove, and the other pressed to where he was slick and wet.

His fever had only lasted two horrible days instead of three, he was surprised to discover. He was still weakened when it was over—the meal he'd ordered at the start barely touched—and he had once again forgotten to stuff himself in the days before the heat had consumed him. But perhaps because Mattin had asked for food at the beginning of his fever, on his day of rest, Elbi knocked on his door and handed him a basket of sweets from the kitchen and told him to get better soon. She didn't mention the gloves. Mattin silently thanked the fae for that.

In the autumn, Mattin forgot his cloak yet again before his breakfast meeting with Arden and Mil—with the king and his husband—and was given Mil's to borrow, which did not help Mattin scowl any less as a headache plagued him through the day, although he did appreciate the cloak and tried to be careful with it. He'd already cost them a pair of gloves, though he'd never brought up the matter like the coward he was; he wasn't going to take a cloak from them too.

But Mil didn't ask for the cloak's return, and Arden softly requested some of the old Canamorra scrolls from the library while handing Mattin a slice of apple tart, and then another slice, and finally an apple itself for Mattin to take to the library with him, and while Mattin was there, he received a note from Arden with an additional question about Canamorra history. The paper was crisp but Mattin would have sworn Arden had worn the paper close to his skin because Arden's scent filled the cubby Mattin had climbed into to dig through ancient records.

Then he'd found what Arden had last asked for—the copy of a copy of a copy of drawing of a tapestry long since lost to time, which depicted one of the ancient Canamorra on the day of their hand-fasting. A wedding portrait that was still so beautiful, even as a copy of a copy of a copy, that Mattin curled up in the cubby on Mil's cloak to stare at it, with the fur at his cheek and Arden's letter in his pocket.

Master Arlylian, Arden had addressed him, always using Mattin's earned rank at the library as if aware Mattin worried over being taken seriously, being a Master Keeper so young. Mattin liked that.

He liked it when Mil called him *Sass* too although he could never tell Mil he did because Mil would be smug. Mil thought Mattin had spirit, even though Mattin really didn't. Mattin was dusty and quite boring in addition to his plainness.

He reread Arden's note as took the clasps out of his hair, then ate his apple and felt almost at peace as he made his way through an account of the hand-fasting in question. He didn't know why when nothing of the account was exactly peaceful. The early Canamorra had seized power quite forcefully, something seemingly at odds with the yearning and passion in the stories of that hand-fasting. What Mattin would have assumed was a political alliance was, to the Canamorra, a romance to make Mattin blush and sigh as he read it and reread it.

Canamorra would give their loves anything they asked for, up to and including an entire country. That was what Mattin felt was beneath the story.

He had no idea why Arden would need these records, or why he needed them now, or how Mattin was going to discuss them with Arden without looking at Mil and wondering if Mil was often taken as many had imagined the first Canamorra taking his beloved, how he was going to look at them both and not imagine himself taken as well.

When the first *pull* from his lower body came—the first sharp enough to make him notice—it was with only quiet surprise and then delight that he'd spotted his fever coming for once. He wished he'd noticed enough to start eating more days ago, but at least it explained why he was so tired and why his pretty hair clasps had pained him. He scooped up the scrolls and climbed out of the cubby before gathering Mil's cloak about him and walking to the king's room.

Arden and Mil were not there, although the guards let Mattin in. Mattin frowned over that a bit, but then another pull hit him, harder than before, and he had to lean against the wall to catch his breath and get his legs to work again. When he recovered, he set the scrolls on their table, a little startled to notice the table held a bowl overflowing with fat, luscious apples and a basket of buns and nut cakes from the kitchen that it hadn't held that morning.

Arden and Mil wouldn't begrudge Mattin either, he knew, but still hesitated. Then his stomach growled with enough force to feel nearly as bad as the tugging, pulling, growing, inexorable need from his lower body. He ended up stuffing a nut cake—two cakes—in his mouth so the guards wouldn't see, and taking an additional apple and pastry with him as he made his way back to his room.

In the winter, Mil unexpectedly took Mattin and Cael with him on a tour of the new barracks for the unattached palace guards, and sat Mattin down next to him to eat a meal with all of them. It was plainer fare than the nobles ate, but Mattin emptied his bowl of stew and half of the plate of bread and butter that Cael insisted she didn't want, and then ate the other half when Mil said he didn't want any either.

Arden told him his brother had been practicing his needlework and had made Arden a chair cushion he didn't need, and offered it to Mattin for his office.

For a cushion Arden didn't need, it smelled of him quite a lot, and of Mil as well, much more than the cloak that Mattin had shoved under his bed and never returned to Mil out of fear of Mil finding out that Mattin had drooled and mouthed at the fur lining while rubbing his small Blessed cock against it, his nose full of the scent of the king, of Mil, while he tried to fill his emptiness with his fingers.

Even thinking of it was enough to make Mattin unable to meet Mil's eyes.

Nonetheless, Mattin piled both onto his bed that evening when he realized the heaviness in his limbs meant his fever was coming on. The cushion and the cloak, and the gloves too, and half a dozen spiced biscuits that Arden said had come from his sister Jola's house.

The items helped make a nest, of course, but Mattin didn't think about that. Not then, and not while he was face down in the cushion and frigging himself with a too-large glove, and not later when he cleaned everything before hiding it all beneath his bed.

He spent his day after in his room without much protest, mostly because Cael had mentioned something of it recently, on account of some relative of hers, and how hard lust-fevers could be on the body. It was pleasant to spend a day lounging in the bath or in bed with a book he chose to read and not one he felt he ought to. Although he'd been itching to get back to work by the time he left his room in search of dinner.

Mattin had never had a fever go so well and thought he understood why so many other Blesseds didn't mind them so much. He could have done without the sweating and writhing and the sounds he sometimes heard himself making, but at least no one else witnessed those.

He went to breakfast the next day as usual, and only blushed faintly when Arden poured sugared almonds into his palm and Mil pushed his cup toward him. If Mattin kept his gaze on his tea, he could imagine they were *his* Gifted watching intently as he nibbled almonds and drank tea with honey and milk. He could imagine it even when he wasn't staring at his cup, and decided he ought to keep his visit short, since his day of rest after his fever had not cooled his blood enough. Only to then linger at their table anyway, inhaling heat and strength and the plain soap they still used even though Arden as king might have had anything.

Mattin thought of offering them some of his soap, although neither of them likely wanted to smell of mint, or chamomile, or lilies. But he could imagine those scents on them, traces left behind from Mattin's hands or from wherever they had touched him. Mattin used oils on his skin to leave it softer, so they might also smell of that, and the scent of him with them and how Mattin would use them would soak into their bedding along with Mattin's slick. Like a nest. Like the only nest worth having. Mattin wouldn't want to leave it. He wouldn't want them to leave it. He could call them to his nest like a real Blessed would, and they would take him, one at a time or together. However Mattin wanted, as many times as he wanted, like the gifts from the fae they were.

"More?" Arden's lovely voice broke into Mattin's thoughts. Mattin turned to him, still lost in his dream, altogether too warm as Arden swept a look over his face.

"More?" Mattin returned, certain he would always want more but unsure how Arden knew that.

"You don't seem satisfied," Arden declared, the firelight hitting the silver in his hair. He had so many more years than Mattin. So much more experience. Mattin must seem an awkward youth to him. To both of them.

Mattin looked to Mil, no less confused when Mil, unlike Mattin, seemed very satisfied indeed. Almost smug.

"Near ravenous I'd say," Mil offered in response to Arden. "I'm familiar with the expression," he added pointedly. Bruises along one side of his throat had the shape of bites, of a mouth.

Arden placed a slice of a hothouse peach in Mattin's palm. It was warm from Arden's hands and dripping. He gave the rest of the peach to Mil.

"You also seem hungry, my love," he murmured, and smiled when Mil mumbled under his breath, though clearly meaning to be heard, that he was *fucking starving and Arden knew it*. But Mil watched Mattin eat the slice he was given and then discreetly lick his fingers clean before he sank his teeth into what was left of the stone fruit. He was nearly growling.

The juice went everywhere, down Mil's chin and between his fingers. Mattin found himself studying his cup of tea again and fighting not to squirm when the pit was discarded and Arden tugged Mil to him by his shirt collar to kiss him with their mouths open. A kiss that made Mil groan. A kiss Mattin could taste on his own tongue, still warm from Arden's hand.

"Not fair," Mil complained quietly when the kiss was over, as if he were in Mattin's place.

Arden kissed him again. Mattin thought it was meant to be soothing. Mil did not seem soothed. Mattin certainly wasn't. He should not have lost himself in thoughts of them. They were happy as they were.

He excused himself shortly after that, resolving that from now on he would spend a day of rest after his fevers in his room, and then another day hiding in his office in the library so that he wouldn't forget himself at their table again, or ruin the seats of any more of his pants.

He also resolved to stay far away from peaches.

He had never even especially cared for peaches. Perhaps he really wasn't getting enough to eat. He should work on improving his meals whenever he next had the time.

The time never came. Arden and Mil, together and separately, had taken to bringing Mattin along with them on various errands around the palace and then apologizing for it as if wasn't Mattin's duty and pleasure to help them.

"We wouldn't want to keep you from anyone, Sass," Mil said once while watching Mattin nibble bits of toffee that Mil had apparently purchased at a spring fair in the capital.

"If you have anywhere else to be, Keeper Arlylian…" Arden had said, quietly polite, while asking for Mattin's help in choosing tea blends for his sister and then insisting Mattin take some as well for his trouble. It was not trouble for Mattin to be around either of them. Not in the sense Arden meant.

If there was any trouble, it was in trying not to embarrass himself simply because they were kind, or smelled good, or shared the soft intimacy of their mornings with him as if trying to confuse him. A sitting room with a small table and a cozy fire was not like the comfort of a nest, nor did it hold the passion of one, but it felt so, sometimes, and Mattin was finding it more and more difficult to tear himself away.

Blessed – Part Two

HE TRAVELED TO THE Arlylian territory to visit his family at the end of summer and was glad for the chance to see his loved ones, and to clear his head away from the palace and the confusing, maddening, wonderful royal couple. He even stayed longer than his usual visit of a few weeks so he could witness a cousin's hand-fasting. The festivities were merry and the wine plentiful enough that Mattin could look on the happy pairing without too much of an ache in his chest. But truthfully, he'd been ready to return home before he'd even unpacked his trunks upon arrival.

The voyage down the river to the capital was endless, the weather too wet and cold and then too hot. Mattin got to his room in the palace late at night and slept past the time when he should have gone to meet with Arden and Mil over breakfast. But, having been gone, he had nothing to bring to them, and since his movements were slow with exhaustion, he decided to save his energy for the work sure to be waiting for him on his desk in his office. He likely hadn't been missed anyway. Another Master Keeper would have sat in on the council meetings and could have answered Cael's questions.

The assistants were pleased to see him, although they kept trying to offer him meals and tea despite how Mattin insisted he was still queasy from his oddly rough boat trip. He accepted the tea at least when his mouth felt dry as a bone, but then it was so hot that he had to wait until it was cool and the bitterness kept him from having more than a sip.

The fever hit him hard that evening, when he was the only one, or hoped he was the only one, left in the library. He staggered outside, probably not locking the doors behind him, and made it to his room only because the path was familiar.

He shook and moaned and ached for three full, horrible days, waking up more than once in his makeshift nest on the floor by the bed, trying to take comfort in gloves and a cushion and a cloak that only smelled like him and Blessed-wet and the oil that he'd reached for when his wet hadn't been enough.

He kept to his room the fourth day despite the gnawing in his stomach, his throat constricting when *Cael* was the one to knock on his door and ask if he was well.

One could not leave Cael of the Rossick on the other side of a closed door, so he answered, begging her to wait while he dressed. But that or the rawness of his voice must have alarmed her, because she ordered food for him without asking, and left a message for him with the meal tray, to come and see her the following day—and, if possible, to visit with the king and his husband sooner than that.

The note also suggested that, if not possible, Mattin ought to visit them sooner anyway.

Mattin had never been in the king's rooms in the evening hours but didn't think Cael's words should be ignored. He bathed several times, cold scrubs at first, and then a longer soak in hot water after he'd eaten. His hair was in two simple braids, which had taken most of his strength, and he wore a heavy robe and pants. Putting those on had taken the rest of it.

He gave the guards at the king's door at wary look but they didn't indicate he ought to turn around and go back to his room, so he forced himself to keep walking.

Arden was probably disappointed with him for the unexpected time away. Mattin was supposed to have been gone three weeks at most but then had spent an additional half a week in his room. He must have been needed, and though Mattin took a bit of vicious pleasure in being the only librarian the king relied on, Arden and Mil should have been able to work with his temporary replacement. Perhaps whichever Keeper had been chosen hadn't understood Mil and Arden the way Mattin did.

Which was a horribly presumptuous thought to have as he was about to step into their private quarters unannounced after disappointing them. He cleared his throat loudly to give them some warning, and then said, "I'm sorry, but Cael told me I ought to come see you," as though his heart wasn't racing and his cheeks weren't flushed.

They were at their table, at dinner, in undershirts and pants and not a single piece of armor. Much like they were in the mornings, only they looked far more tired in the glimpse Mattin got before they were both up out of their seats and ushering him to the seat at the table closest to the fireplace. Their hands were big and very warm and pressed to him in many places for several confusing, torturous moments.

They were hale and healthy, and Mattin was almost grateful they were too busy fussing to notice how he could not look away from them. They did not seem to have the same opinion of Mattin's appearance that he had of theirs, but they couldn't be expected to have missed him as he had missed them.

Still, Mattin did wish for a moment that they thought him beautiful, or at least would not speak of how horrible he must look.

"What did they do to him?" Mil asked Arden above Mattin's head. "Hasn't eaten in a week, I'll bet."

"I ate today," Mattin objected, feeling very silly for speaking at all when they both ignored him.

"Probably his first real meal since he left home," Arden replied to his husband, then sat down to study Mattin closely.

Mattin's face was no doubt blazing red. A plate was nudged in front of him, loaded with potatoes, carrots, and venison covered in gravy. Mattin had to swallow to keep from openly salivating.

Mil picked up Mattin's hand and placed a fork in it. "Eat, please, and then tell us about your trip."

Really, Mattin should have said something or glared at them both—handing him a fork as if he didn't know how to eat—but the food did look good, and they certainly had plenty so he wasn't denying them anything. He did manage to ask if they were sure and caught Arden with a smile on his face that was so indulgent, Mattin had to glance at Mil to see what Mil had done to cause it.

Mil grunted, "Eat," at him, which was the only answer Mattin got. With both of them looking at him it felt like an order, so Mattin took the smallest possible piece of potato and ate it, pretending the first hint of spice and butter didn't make him weak.

"Very delicate," Mil commented in a rough voice. "Very proper. Eat more, please, if you'd be so kind."

Mattin put more potato in his mouth just to keep in his sighs of longing. "I don't mean to make you worry," he said softly when he could.

"And yet," Arden answered gravely, "nearly a month you've been gone. Then you return pale as a ghost except for the color in your cheeks. It's good to see you again, dear h—Master Arlylian, but I think seeing you has made us worry more."

"Not that it helped, hearing that you'd returned but that you were *unwell*." Mil pronounced the word as though he'd been practicing saying it instead of whatever he actually wanted to say. So many beat-of-fours complained Mil couldn't be diplomatic, but he could when he wanted to.

Mattin glanced up, then went very still as Mil wiped a bit of gravy from his cheek for him. Mil licked the gravy from his fingers, casual as anything. Mattin turned quickly to Arden, then dropped his gaze entirely to his plate when Arden's attention was too much.

The potatoes were all gone. Mattin frowned.

"Carrots next?" Arden suggested. Except Arden of the Canamorra's suggestions were actually polite orders.

Mattin nodded and wondered how long the look he had just interrupted would haunt him. "You've both been well? It takes a while for news to reach Arlylian territory, so I wasn't sure that... I mean, I hoped that you were well."

"Oh, some of the usual beat-of-four families kicking up a fuss over any old thing." Arden spoke lightly of something that was a real problem and, if Cael was to be believed, a danger. "Some of them posturing. Some wanting something else from me. And some... well, not a topic you need to fret over at this moment in time, Mattin Arlylian."

Mattin opened his eyes, which seemed to have fallen closed, and resumed eating carrots, although he didn't care for them and drowned them in gravy first. A little too late, he realized this was probably Arden's dinner he was eating and glanced over. Arden responded by dropping a dinner roll onto Mattin's plate and smiling.

He had a very charming smile, even if the scar down his cheek made him look rather forbidden and illicit, like a bandit of old. Mattin turned to Mil, who smiled at him as well. Mil's warm smiles just made Mil look even more handsome, as though he could be easily charmed, which wasn't at all true. Although when he *was* charmed, it was usually by his husband or Arden's young niece. Or Mattin when he supposedly sassed them.

But Mattin had come here to say something and it had nothing to do with dinner or smiles. He turned back to his food while he tried to remember what it was. The gravy was quite good. He sopped it up with the roll, then wiped his hands on a napkin, which made Mil sigh for reasons unknown.

After not eating, not as he should have, for several days, and then his fever days where he had not swallowed even a scrap, so much food made Mattin's stomach hurt, but also made him aware of how tired he was. The fire was incredibly warm. Arden and Mil, on either side of him, were hot as well, although Mattin shouldn't have been able to feel their body heat where he was. He might have imagined it. Or it was his fever lingering in odd ways.

Arden handed him a cup which held wine mixed with fruit juice, and Mattin was so very thirsty. He emptied it and put it down, then closed his eyes.

"Mil, my love, are your plans for tomorrow still to ride out to look over the back sections of the old palace wall?"

The question was voiced softly over Mattin's head. Arden must have bathed this evening; he smelled of plain soap and maybe a bit of wine. No leather on him now. Just Arden-scent and traces of bathwater.

Mil must have been busy until late. No soap scent around him, but clean sweat at his neck and then spiced tea on his breath, as if he'd needed the tea to keep going. "Aye, but I'll be back in time for the council meeting. Wouldn't leave you to handle that bunch alone. Will you be there too, Sass? Or do you need more time to rest?"

Mattin gave a start, then put his hands to his cheeks as he realized he had been sitting between them with his eyes closed, inhaling their scents. He could not look up. Not even if Cael herself were to ask him to. He hoped they thought he'd fallen asleep, but even that was beyond rude. Anyway, he doubted he was so lucky. They'd noticed. Of course, they would have.

"I'm sorry." He'd known he would miss them when he left, but he hadn't thought about what it would be like to return to them, especially so close to a fever. "I didn't mean to... I'm sorry. I forgot my fever was near. That's why I was late. I'm sorry." That was what he'd come here to say.

"We didn't," Mil revealed easily, and then paused in reaching for more wine when Mattin squawked.

"*What*? What do you mean you didn't?"

"We didn't forget your fever was due," Arden explained. "But you were with your family, so we assumed they would make sure you ate enough. I can see now that we'll have to do better next time since they obviously won't."

"Did you think we'd be mad you had your lust-fever and couldn't visit?" Mil briefly looked hurt. "Why would we?"

Mattin blinked dry eyes, then turned on Arden. "You... remembered my fever was due?"

Saying it out loud was a mistake. Humiliation stung him as he realized they had remembered his own fever schedule better than he had. That was followed by a sweeping, all-over heat to imagine them thinking of Mattin and a last-fever at the same time, even if they'd only done so abstractly.

Arden met Mattin's stare without hesitation. "We rely on you, and we like to consider you a friend, and we worry when you don't appear."

Now Mattin could not look anywhere else. "Oh."

"And you don't have anyone you'll let care for you," Mil grumbled. "And you never remember to prepare in the days leading up to it."

"Too used to ignoring his body's needs," Arden agreed. "A bad habit among librarians, I hear."

Mattin briefly and spitefully wondered if Arden had been an outguard fond of tupping library assistants but didn't ask.

"It's fine," he said instead. "I'm fine, despite that."

Mil scoffed rudely. "You don't see yourself after, Sass. You needed caring for. Still do, and something better than what can be offered from a distance. No partners in sight for you yet? Not a one has caught your eye?"

Mattin had no idea how the subject had gotten to his fever-partners, or lack thereof, but faced Mil just to glare at him and ignored the conciliatory, "Now, Sass," Mil tried to offer.

"Maybe you don't want any kind of partner, in or out of a fever?" Arden said, or asked, Mattin wasn't sure. They were both staring at him now.

Mattin's stomach gurgled again. How it could do that with him already stuffed full, he had no idea.

"I keep telling you I am plain and small and not interesting," he huffed, although he wasn't sure he'd ever told them anything like that. He accepted the second dinner roll from Arden with another huff, then tore it to pieces over his plate. "It wasn't... the palace wasn't safe for a long time. All the years of fighting.... People were terrified, and nobody was.... It's not like it is now, or was before. So I'm not very experienced with any sort of... *that*." He only had to explain this to them because they were both too confident and handsome to understand his predicament. "Not casually and definitely not for several days of me... being how the Blessed are in their fevers."

"We didn't mean to embarrass you, Sass."

Mattin gave Mil a huff too. He didn't see what else anyone would be *but* embarrassed to have their lust-fevers the subject of conversation between the king and his husband.

Well, *aroused*, but Mattin was not going to think of that here if he could help it. He had already spent the last few days imagining other things between the king and his husband. Like himself. And it was not a thought to make it stop throbbing between his legs or to keep him from wanting to put hand over his cock underneath a robe that now did not seem heavy enough.

"So…" Arden was being delicate, which was somehow touching and alarming together, "it's more that you don't *know*, and not that you don't *want*?"

Mattin darted a look up, saw the two of them exchanging a glance, then dropped his gaze again. "To be… like *that* in front of someone." He knew what he was like, even if the fever days were a blur. Sweating and moaning and crying out until his throat was raw. Waking to bruises and a sore body and all sorts of damage to whatever had happened to be in his way. Mattin during a fever was, unfortunately, rather wild. "I'd probably startle them. Or repulse them."

Mil made a noise, a stifled growl that carried into his words. "I highly doubt that."

"I think whoever you choose would be deeply honored, Mattin Arlylian, and delighted to be chosen."

Mattin's gaze came up.

Arden was so serious. "If you ever need help, if you ever want it, you're welcome to ask us."

The strangled sound Mattin made might have been a growl too. A pathetic sort of a growl that led to Mil pushing his own wine toward him as though Mattin had something stuck in his throat.

Arden had not looked away. "Or just one of us if that makes you more comfortable. I won't be offended when you choose Mil."

Mattin swung around to stare at Mil.

"Well, now," Mil said, blinking several times before looking at his husband with his eyebrows raised.

"I'm not saying he would," Arden explained, gentle with the both of them, "but Mattin—Keeper Arlylian, is proper, and I'm the king, aren't I?"

Mattin turned back to him. "You'd be needed elsewhere," he admitted softly.

Arden gave him a crooked grin. "Exceptions would be made for the Blessed, everyone knows that. No one is going to spit in the face of a fae gift, no matter how much they dislike or hate the king, or require something from him."

"But I wouldn't..." Mattin started, then fell silent because he had no idea what he meant to say. He would have been angry if they offered out of pity, but they had just called him a friend and he knew that was true because they allowed him to see them like this, private and half-undressed, enjoying their meals in peace. "I'm sure you would be very good partners," he declared at last, with manners enough that Mil should have teased him. Mattin decided to study the torn pieces of roll on his plate. "But I'm not much of a Blessed." A real Blessed wouldn't care about more than being pleased during their fever. Mattin suspected that getting that from them and then losing it when the fever had ended would hurt worse than a fever spent alone.

For one moment, Arden's hand covered his on the table. "The offer wasn't meant to upset you."

"I know." Mattin *did* know it. "But...."

"Just think on it," Mil added, gruff. "Know that it's available to you, rather than suffering. Or, if you only want more things to aid with your fevers, let us know, and we'll get you what you need."

Mattin frowned and then finally, much, much too late, realized that he had been given gifts for his nest on purpose. They'd loaned their scents to help ease his pains. The best and worst thing he could have been given.

"Scent matters to the Blessed," Arden said while Mattin burned with humiliation and flattered pleasure over their thoughtfulness. Arden's manner was manner-of-fact, because of course, he was experienced and knew how best to help a Blessed through a fever.

"Now, you see." Mattin said at last, because they both were watching him in a way that suggested they were anxiously waiting for him to speak. "how much of a poor Blessed I am."

"Poor Blessed, my ass." Mil took Mattin's hand and held it in his. Like Arden's, the touch lasted only a moment. "You're fine as you are. It's just that when you should have been learning about and trying these things, the palace was a bloody mess, and trust is a hard thing to grant. Maybe you should have gone back to your family territory then to wait it all out, and learned there. But... I have to say, I'm glad you stuck, Sass. I'm very glad you're here."

"Oh," Mattin murmured again, quite foolishly. That seemed to be all he could say, except for an even softer, "Thank you," a few moments later when he got his breathing even again.

"Would you like some tea?" Mil asked a bit awkwardly when the silence went on and Mattin had trouble raising his head. When he finally did, they were both watching him carefully. "We can get you some tea."

Mattin's heart thumped uncomfortably against his ribs, or seemed to.

"Thank you," he said, which Mil took as a yes, and got up to ask someone to bring tea before returning to Mattin's side. "I'm sorry. I'm still very tired and you're both..."

"Pushy?" Arden quirked a smile.

"Wonderful," Mattin finished. "It's embarrassing, really. I can't... It was especially difficult this time, you see. Harder than before." Because the two of them hadn't been there to make sure he ate more, or to give him trinkets worn close to their bodies.

"We'll do better next time," Arden promised. "Even if you're far away."

That was not their job or their role. But they knew that and had said it anyway.

"Just think on it," Mil said again. The nobles at court who thought him a brute without gentleness did not know him. He put a new roll on Mattin's plate and then put more gravy next to it. "Eat now, though, yes?"

"All right," Mattin agreed quietly, still burning, and felt his heart thump again when Arden began to talk to Mil about the old palace wall so Mattin could fret tiredly, and eat, and inhale the scents he had missed so much it had pained him even before his fever.

But that was something to fret over more and in greater depth later. Or never. But probably later, when he was rested and had time.

Blessed – Part Three

"If His Highness is so preoccupied by the concerns of the court, perhaps he should consider finding a new consort suited to handle such matters."

The words rang in Mattin's ears for hours after he left the council chamber. The beat-of-fours who persisted in troubling Arden had grown tired of petty complaints and had now issued a challenge that could not be ignored.

There was even some truth in it, though Mattin hated to admit it. The country was recovering from decades of war between the noble families. Arden as king they could accept—at least most of them—but Mil was no diplomat, and certainly—and proudly—not from a noble family. It didn't matter that he was a hero who had helped save the capital; if peace was to be maintained, Arden would need to make another alliance.

That not all alliances were marriages didn't seem to matter in Mattin's thoughts. He could not stop frowning during his frozen walk in the snow from the council chamber to his office, and then could not be still, although his feet dragged.

He expected Arden and Mil to be upset in private at the mere suggestion that anyone could possibly stand at Arden's side as Mil did, but though they had been serious, in their way, they hadn't been worried as Mattin was. Nor had they been saddened or dismayed or furious. They had been… amused, almost, at the idea of an alliance with some beat-of-four and the possibility of a new spouse in their bed.

That this also meant that they would now be unlikely to help Mattin through his fevers, well, Mattin didn't have time to think on it and they hadn't spoken of it. Only that they would need to marry—to ally with but possibly eventually marry—a suitable noble. Someone with an ancient family name of four beats. Someone who could accept and maybe love Mil as well as Arden. Someone who belonged with them in the big bed Mattin imagined they had beyond the second set of curtains leading out of their sitting room. A nest they would not welcome just anyone into. A place that not many deserved, not as far as Mattin was concerned.

And Arden wanted Mattin to help them find this person. Or so it had seemed with Arden and Mil watching Mattin frown and fret and try not to snarl like a hungry Blessed in a fever, and serving him tea to calm him, and saying, "We trust your decision, Mattin of the Arlylian. Who would you choose for us?"

"Who would you put in our bed?" Arden had added alone.

As if Mattin wanted to do that, put someone else in their bed, choose someone else for them.

But he couldn't deny them and the country was at stake. So he trekked through the winter snows to his office and poured through library records of the other beat-of-four families and made list after list of suitable candidates, of Gifted and Blessed and those in between and some not even a little fae-touched.

He was at it for days, until his vision began to swim and he was sure the assistants had seen how upset he was and pitied him.

A pain in his stomach was making itself known when Elbi rapped on his door and came in with a tray of food that Mattin hadn't asked for. He accepted it politely and meant to get to it when he was done, but it was pheasant with wine and mushrooms, which was a personal favorite, so he stopped long enough to eat it, and then the breads and pastries that came with it.

Another tray replaced it hours later, this one heavy with cake and tea. He finished that too while scowling at histories of families that contained far too much scandal to be suitable for Arden and Mil's political needs. He didn't know how to make a list for their other needs. He would have to ask them what they liked, if Mil liked to only be taken by Arden or if he also did some taking. If they wanted someone as strong and tall as they were, or someone small and weak. Someone simple and austere in tastes, or fond of flowers and clasps and pretty things. They probably would want someone sensible who could be trusted to feed himself or to get enough sleep. Someone who, if he had lust-fevers, prepared for them and knew how to call sweetly and beckon Gifted to his side.

Someone who would make them smile and allow Arden to feel safe enough to show those smiles. Someone to be patient as they fussed, and snap only a little when they went too far. Who would love them in no time at all, and fit snugly between them in sleep or out of it.

Someone who would not care for Mattin breathing them in or sharing their table.

Mattin's lips curled. A tiny sound rumbled in his chest. The tea made him sweat, so he didn't add more logs to the fire in his office fireplace.

Then he got too cold and gave up, trudging to his room in the dark of night without his cloak which he had forgotten again.

He threw the list he'd made in the fire the next day and started over. His head ached from his fitful, restless night. He let his fire go out and was vaguely aware of an ache in his bones as he neatly wrote out a final list of candidates.

The rap on the door was another assistant, a new one whose name he didn't know, with a tray of toast and jam. Breakfast foods.

Mattin had not taken breakfast with Arden and Mil—the king and his husband, they must stay the king and his husband—for several days now, he realized, and longed to be at their table, where the heat of a fire did not plague him. They would be there, of course, the king and his husband, Arden and Mil, to watch him and fuss over him and offer him fruit and speak of hunger and... he had to give them the list.

Once they had it, once they chose.... Mattin ended the thought there.

He folded up the paper and ignored the toast, knowing he'd find it later and eat it, cold or stale, without tasting it. Then he headed out, grateful for the snow to cool his stinging face and slow his rushing blood.

He wondered absently where he'd left his cloak. People gave him strange looks as he passed, perhaps for that, or his lack of winter gloves, or for the sweat at his hairline and the back of his neck.

He stopped in a corridor halfway to his room to unfold the paper and look at his list again. Once Mil and Arden chose someone, Mattin would probably never know them as fever partners. Or anything else, but he hadn't been offered anything else. Only that.

He started to walk again, the paper crumpled in one fist, and startled a passing guard with a growl that rumbled from him with no warning.

The sound shocked him into stopping to give a flustered apology. Then he hurried away, flushed to his ears, pulling at the buttons on his vest until it was loose enough for him to shrug away. The cold still did not reach him. It didn't take the low pull in his belly for him to realize what was happening.

He had growled at a guard. Word would get out. Mil would tease him.

The second pull hit him at the thought of Mil's smile, and Mattin dropped to his knees in the snow. This pull was sharp and hot and *slow* because Mil would tease him but Mil would also fuck him if he asked. If Mattin sighed Mil's name and curled his fingers to summon him like a real Blessed would, Mil would answer. Mil was bigger than Mattin, so much bigger, larger even than Arden, and he would crush Mattin and fill him, and smile, satisfied and smug when he turned to his husband. Because Arden *would* be there. Mattin couldn't beckon one without the other, not for a heat, not for a fever in his blood and such an ache that he could barely walk around it.

He imagined if he demanded it as was his right as a Blessed, they would take him together, stretch him so wide he would never feel empty again. If they were his Gifted, he could make such a request and fit perfectly between them while they obeyed and ravished him.

Mattin bit his lip hard but it did not keep him from moaning on his knees right there in the corridor.

"Are you all right?" someone asked very far away. Mattin stared at them blankly for too long, then nodded and got to his feet, legs shaking, his clothes wet with more than snow, snarling a little when the stranger tried to help him up because he didn't want that person to touch him. He gulped around another apology but could feel the snarl lingering on his face. He had ruined his pants but couldn't seem to feel upset about it, in the same way that he had forgotten his approaching fever once again but wasn't bothered, because they'd sent him food. They had remembered not only that Mattin would need to eat, but his favorite foods.

And now they would marry and he would never know them unless he....

He stumbled to a stop at the door to the king's rooms, confused to be there and then aware of himself enough again to be embarrassed at the stunned expressions on the faces of the guards.

Mattin glanced down at himself, half-undressed, dirtied and wet from snow at his knees and then... and then wet elsewhere, sticky at his backside and down his thighs. His clothes were too fine for the winter, too thin, as Mil would say. Mattin's arousal would be obvious who anyone who glanced down. He imagined his eyes were fever-bright, his cheeks as red as his lips, which he kept biting because he kept wanting to moan.

The stickiness against his skin would have bothered him at another time. Like mess. Like the juice of a peach, it had to be dealt with right away before it became a problem.

He thought of Arden's hand, and Mil's mouth, and bite marks and deep kisses, and felt his knees wobble.

He dropped his head and said, "Excuse me," in his politest voice before hurrying into the waiting room outside Arden's study. No one was using it to wait today. He thanked the fae for that.

Behind him, one of the guards called for the other one to run, and quickly. Mattin paused for that, worried that perhaps there was a threat or some danger, but they'd let him in, so he continued to the study, also unoccupied, and then with no announcement, into the sitting room.

That was silent and cold. Of course it was. Arden and Mil were out, and would likely be out all day. Mattin was silly for being here. He didn't have much time left before he embarrassed himself further.

Without the fire lit, the room was chilly, although he noted the goosebumps on his arms without feeling them. He didn't know when he'd rolled up his sleeves. In the snow, possibly, on his hands and knees, when he'd nearly dropped the list.

The list was damp and stained now. Mattin frowned at it, feeling another snarl build that he forced down. He put the cursed list on the table and let go.

He took a breath. He had to be calm, although he couldn't recall why. The air in the sitting room remained cool. He could smell Arden and Mil but only faintly, and wondered if they would mind if he took a cushion back to his room, or maybe a shirt they might have lying around.

He inhaled again and turned blindly toward the stronger scent of them. Of Gifted. Of Arden and Mil. Of *his* Gifted.

Then he was beyond another curtain, in another room, and the scent was so powerful that he put his hands over his mouth to muffle his whimpers. Before him, like something from his fever dreams, was a bed. A large bed, covered in blankets and furs that had been tossed over it as though Mil and Arden had woken late or been in a rush that morning. There was no fire in the fireplace by the bed but Mattin could feel one beneath his skin. He licked his upper lip and then sank his teeth into his lower one, which was already bruised.

He should not be there. If he stayed, he should at least not touch anything unless they said he could.

But they would let him. Perhaps they would even let him burrow into that nest.

Oh, but he had stained his clothes. That was a worry. He disliked mess. He *normally* disliked mess, especially waking up to it. If he got in that bed…

Mattin stopped. He wasn't supposed to get into that bed. He remembered that much before getting distracted once again. His clothes were too tight and soaked now with snow and slick, so much slick from the thought of Arden and Mil. *Oh,* he had thought of them, and how he would have them both no matter what Arden imagined. They would take turns and use him together and then take turns again. Mattin needed that and they would give it to him. They had promised they would if he asked. He was not much of a Blessed, but he could do that. Politely, and not how he wanted to, but he was not a beast.

His clothes were dirty. That was what he was trying to remember, and he didn't want his dirty clothes in their nest even if his clothes smelled of how much he desired his Gifted. It was a very good nest. Mattin couldn't have made one better, a firm mattress and soft bedding, with furs soothing against his skin, and the scent of the two of them now mingling with his, faint with lilies. He rubbed his cheek against one of the furs as Mil pushed the curtains back and stopped dead in the doorway.

"Fuck me," Mil muttered without moving. "Fuck me hard. He's just... Arden. Please."

Mattin scowled at him and then at Arden who pushed past Mil only to also stop by the door to stare.

Arden opened his mouth, then closed it. He glanced around the room until he found Mattin's clothes on the floor. The alarm or fear on his face, whatever had him and Mil panting as though they'd run here, seemed to fall away. He inhaled and then said softly, "Is that a nest you've made in our bed, Mattin Arlylian?"

"Your nest for me," Mattin corrected him, then, just for a moment, worried. "Isn't it?"

"*Yes,*" they both agreed immediately, nodding until Mattin sank into the furs again.

"Smells of you," Mattin revealed, tensing at the hoarse noise from Mil. He peered with blurry eyes at the two of them looking back at him, then wriggled to sit up, getting as far as on his hands and knees when the brush of fur over sensitive skin made him whine with how good it was. He rolled his hips to feel that again and closed his eyes as he curled back into the fur, running his palms over the silky surface until he found the ticklish patch over his ribs. Then he ran his palm over that too, sliding it down to the curve of his backside and then beneath his body to the steadily growing puddle before reopening his eyes to find his Gifted. Fur teased his cock as he twitched his hips up. His fingers did not quite reach where Mattin wanted them to go. Not as deeply as he wished they would.

The sound Mil made this time was more choked.

"Did you have Mil here this morning?" Mattin asked Arden in a throaty, husky voice. Arden used plain soap and sturdy mugs, yet had such perfectly soft bedding. He had done that for Mil, and now Mattin. He would give them all he had. He would give Mattin all he wanted. A whole country if Mattin asked, Mattin thought dizzily, although all he wanted now was cock and inched his knees apart. "I can smell it."

"Fuck. Me." Mil pronounced each word distinctly.

"Me first," Mattin insisted. "I'm so hot."

Mil let out a shaky breath. "Of course, you are, Sass. This is your lust-fever. This is… you in a lust-fever. In our bed—our nest. *Fuck*. Your nest. It's been waiting for you. *We've* been waiting for you. We just didn't expect—fuck, you're beautiful."

Mattin opened his eyes, which he had closed while pressing his fingertips into tight, soft heat. Mil was closer and still breathing hard, barely seeming aware of Arden behind him hastily removing his armor for him. Mil was the beautiful one, and large, and handsome, and he smelled strong and lovely, and he was so, so big that Mattin's whole lower body tightened and let go with one sudden overwhelming *pull*.

Mattin moaned all the way through it, open and ready now, wet and starving.

"I'm hot," Mattin informed Mil again. "You offered to help me and it… it smells good here and I'm hot, and it, *ah*," he heard his tiny, breathless cry as if it came from someone else. "Ah, there's an ache inside, Mil. Mil, please. I'm ready for you."

Mil's breastplate fell to the floor with a terrible sound that didn't quite cover Arden calling to the guards outside. He shouted something about Cael, and his apologies, and the next few days.

"Is there anything you need, dear heart?" Arden asked when he was done, drawing Mattin's attention to him. Arden's voice was concerned and low. It dragged heat through Mattin's spine and pulled another throbbing spasm from his lower body. He felt wet trickle to his knees and shifted until he was on his elbows. It put his hips higher.

His legs were shaking. His braid fell to one side, damp with sweat. He didn't know where his pretty clothes had gone. He didn't care. He was made of fire and need and emptiness.

"Arden," Mattin complained. "You're too far away."

Mil wasn't. He was close enough now to touch Mattin, and finally did, resting one large hand on the back of Mattin's neck. Mattin pushed into his palm and wished he could purr.

"Oh, you *are* hot, aren't you, poor thing?" Mil said sympathetically, but not doing anything to help. Mattin raised his head to scowl. "Oh, *Sass*," Mil purred for him as if the scowl had pleased. "Is there something particular you'd like us to do?"

Arden was more warmth next to Mattin, more good scent, more heat, another hand on Mattin's bare skin and another solid weight around him like a bookend. He brushed the back of his hand over Mattin's shoulder, then turned his hand to run his palm down Mattin's spine. Mattin tried to get his hips higher and his clever Gifted Arden understood and curved his hand over the source of Mattin's heat. He was hotter than Mattin was, hotter still once his fingers opened Mattin and pushed inside. "What a gift you are to come home to, dear heart. Our Blessed Mattin here in our nest waiting for us. I bet you're as tired of waiting as we are. Ah. You *are*." He pressed deeper and Mattin welcomed his fingers without any resistance. "He wasn't lying, my love."

Mattin nodded with eager, yet annoyed gratitude to be understood at last, then looked to Mil. Arden had fingers inside him and yet Mattin bit his lip and whimpered until Mil said, "None of that now. Whatever you want, Sass. Say it and he'll give it to you. We both will."

He stroked Mattin's cheek before gently tugging Mattin's lip from between his teeth.

His mouth now open, Mattin turned his head to follow the scent of Mil to his cock and nuzzle that before taking the tip into his mouth. It was large. Mattin, unpracticed and hungry, suckled clumsily, pausing to swallow the spit that kept gathering in his mouth and spilling down his chin before pushing forward to try again. He took more, or wanted to, falling back with a moan when Arden moved his hand. Mattin returned almost immediately, sucking hard with a noise that, if Mattin had been able to think, would have made him blush.

Mil grunted. His hand fell into Mattin's hair, tightened painfully, then let go. "Sorry, Sass." He ran an apologetic touch down Mattin's braid that Mattin could barely feel.

Mattin pulled off Mil's cock to gaze at Mil reproachfully.

"Mil." The name and taste were on his tongue. Mattin was not weak, he was *hungry*. "Arden." He pushed back, gasping at the pressure from Arden's fingers alone as they went still deeper, and then were slowly drawn out before Arden slid them back in. Mattin's chest rumbled with another growl. He let it out, then pulled in a shaky breath.

"Sorry, Sass," Mil said again, properly contrite as he took Mattin's braid and wound it around his wrist and tightened his hold again the way Mattin had liked. Mil would hold Mattin in place now, as he should. He had his cock in his other hand and brought it to Mattin's lips and groaned when Mattin surged forward to take as much as he could. He started to say several things, warnings perhaps, worries about the sounds of Mattin's gagging, but he kept his hold on Mattin's hair and let Mattin suck how he liked.

Mattin was vaguely aware of the mess he was making and that he was still burning. But it was a good mess, and having his mouth full soothed him as much as holding Mil's bright, mesmerized gaze while he worked his tongue, and choked, and dribbled spit.

Mil brushed the corners of Mattin's mouth when they grew too wet no matter how often Mattin swallowed. His hand shook, although Mattin didn't know why, and he said things about Mattin's red mouth that drew another long pull of need from deep within Mattin and made him briefly inch away to drop his head and moan. Then Mil took him by the hair and gently pulled him back to his cock and Mattin hummed his gratitude in between licks and swallows.

Arden kept one hand on Mattin's back as if to settle Mattin, but then would not stop tormenting him. *Steadying you*, he said more than once, *readying you for what you'll take*, but Mattin thought it was more that he enjoyed the sight of Mattin with his mouth full while Arden stuffed him with his fingers. Mattin *was* ready. He shook and shuddered, and growled around the head of Mil's cock because he could not fit the rest in his mouth, and every time Mattin coughed and stuttered over taking a breath, Arden kissed his shoulder or the base of his spine and continued his readying.

Mattin was alight. He was raw inside without being used, on fire from the tastes he coaxed from Mil's cock and the slide of Arden's fingers. Mattin finally pulled away from the cock meant for his mouth and pushed back onto Arden's hand with a rough snarl. "I'm so *hot*. You smell good and I'm wet. I'm *messy*. I'm... I'm empty. I don't like it." His mind was *almost* clear. He held to his thoughts for another moment, worrying over something, perhaps that he had not said please, perhaps that Arden was right and he wasn't ready for what he would take, but he wanted it. He wanted so much he was roasting with it, so he put his face to the furs and lifted his hips as high as they could go.

"That's more than ready." Mil said in a rasping, sticky sort of a voice, as if he had some of Mattin's slick in his mouth. He dropped Mattin's braid to pet the top of Mattin's head and the back of his neck before he bent over Mattin to kiss his shoulder where Arden had, and then again to kiss Mattin lower, at the base of his spine.

Slick dripped from Mattin when Arden pulled his fingers out. Mattin sobbed for being even emptier than before, and they both kissed him again, mouths close to where they could be, their breath mingling over overheated, wet skin, which did nothing except make Mattin shiver.

Arden was careful, as though he hadn't moved his hand and his damp fingers to Mattin's thigh, then up to tease Mattin's little cock. "Tell us what you want while you still can, dear heart."

Mil slid his fingers into Mattin, bigger than Arden's but welcomed just as readily. They were both on either side of him, nearly behind him, watching Mattin grow wetter, watching him take Mil's fingers and then Arden's again alongside Mil's, Mil fucking in and out and Arden pressing in as if he knew exactly what Mattin wanted despite what he'd asked. He stroked Mattin's cock slowly, and when Mattin began to shake, said, "*Tell us,*" as an order; a real one, no longer pretending to be polite.

Mattin did not hesitate, too hot to even know what a blush was. "Both—" a cry interrupted him, rising to the ceiling, carrying out into the sitting room and perhaps farther. Arden and Mil moved their fingers together, opening him up with wet sounds that left Mattin even hungrier. Needier. Emptier. "—Both of you." He could not even writhe away from the pleasure because Mil held him in place. It would take Mil no effort to do so, even distracted and panting while he and Arden readied Mattin.

They knew what he wanted or they wanted it too. Mattin arched into the pressure, the lust-fever *pull* that meant his body wanted mess and load upon load of seed and their beautiful cocks pounding into him. He could not bear having that. He couldn't bear not having that. All the while, they did not let up, his Gifted, asking him what he wanted when they knew.

"Both of you." Mattin put his face to the fur and left his lower body to their control. He felt so good, so hot and so empty but so good. They would give him what he needed. "Fuck me."

He demanded it like the Blessed he was and cared only that they obeyed as they should.

Arden was next to him when Mattin opened his eyes, looking so wickedly handsome that Mattin stared at him for a long while before he even realized he *was* staring. With some confusion, Mattin considered the side of Arden's face and then the fireplace in Mil and Arden's sitting room, currently blazing with a toasty fire. Then he studied the table in front of him, laden with quite possibly every fruit the palace greenhouse had to offer as well as a pot of tea and platter full of sweet buns.

There was a cup of tea before him. Mattin had the vague thought that he'd had some tea already, milkier than he usually drank it, but someone had insisted he needed it.

He supposed he did. He was... very tired.

He turned back to Arden for explanation and then jolted, which made Arden put down whatever he was reading to look at him.

Arden was not just next to him. Mattin was pressed against Arden's side from chest to thigh, and while Arden was dressed in an undershirt and pants, Mattin was not. Mattin was wearing a blanket. Or—he looked down—a large towel, with a blanket thrown over his legs.

He turned to Arden again, who stared back at him, interested and warm despite the shadows beneath his eyes that said he was also tired. His hair was damp, so he must have bathed not long ago, which was when Mattin realized that his hair was wet too but wrapped in another towel.

He left Arden to stare at him with that mortifyingly indulgent expression on his face to glance around the rest of the room, but Mil didn't seem to be there.

Mattin was in their rooms but he wasn't.... He'd come here for help, but he couldn't be post-fever. He was tired and confused and hungry, but nowhere near as worn out as he should be.

"Did you... did you not want me?" That was also mortifying, but it was saying the words that made him aware of his hoarse throat and how the rest of his body was somewhat raw.

Very raw. Sore in places and tingling and sensitive in others. But not aching. Not pained.

He recognized this with wonder, then turned back to Arden.

"Not want you?" Arden clucked his tongue.

"I'm sorry," Mattin apologized immediately. "I've never felt this good befo..." He trailed off at Arden's obviously smug expression. "I've never not hurt the next day," he said anyway because Arden should hear it. He had a feeling his face was red but he still felt the fever enough that it meant nothing. "Thank you. I hope I wasn't too much trouble."

Arden snorted softly, then angled his head so Mattin could better see his neck and the four raised lines that Mattin took several moments to recognize as scratches. Arden lifted one of Mattin's hands and raised it to the spot, where Mattin's fingers lined up perfectly.

"Dear heart," Arden was fondly amused, "you had two Gifted with you and we could barely keep up. Trouble? We are blessed indeed."

"You should see the marks on my backside," Mil announced as he pushed aside the curtains that led to the bedroom to enter the sitting room.

Mattin had a sudden, vivid memory of the bed in that room, the furs covering it clumped and wet with spend and Mattin's slick, Mattin's cheek sliding against a place not yet sullied as Mil plowed into him. Arden's hand had been at Mattin's neck, holding him down, not that Mattin had struggled.

Or had he? Mattin's lips curled with a remembered snarl, and then he heard, "*More*," in his voice, before hands went to his hips to move him. Arden ordered Mattin to breathe, as if Mattin would ever forget to do that. Then Mattin was shaking out a gasp and gazing up at nothing as he was filled, and filled, and he couldn't move and did not take in air until just before he heard his voice again, commanding, "*More*," sweet and slow as honey.

Then Mil's remark sank in and Mattin snapped his attention to Mil while Mil calmly took a seat at the table and began to eat.

"I did not scratch your..." Mattin didn't even get a chance to finish before Mil waggled his eyebrows. "Oh no." Mattin turned to Arden, who was no less smug. "Oh *no*."

"Oh yes." Mil nearly purred it. "Sassed us good and proper too. Kept us in line and focused on our work as surely as any Blessed ought to."

Mattin tried to hold in another protest but a squeak emerged.

"Absolutely ruined one of the blankets," Arden revealed. "Mil wants to display it somewhere."

"Wild little thing under all those fancy vests." Mil sighed happily. "More than I ever expected. Think you about killed me when we ran in and found you like that, Sass."

Mattin should not ask. He knew he should not, because they wanted him to. "Like what?" he asked anyway, blushing so much he could feel it through the fever.

"Naked and hungry." Mil's hot stare held Mattin in place, no matter how much he wanted to duck his head against Arden and never look up again.

"Helped yourself to our bed, which was unexpected," Arden added like someone trying to sound thoughtful but who was just as aroused as Mil was. "But a good surprise. Our pretty Blessed waiting for us. I'm sorry it took us so long to get there, and that I had to be sure you were ready."

Mattin wondered with distant hysteria if they expected him to scold them for it. He supposed he should. That was their role and their duty, or would have been, if he'd ever properly asked them to assist him during his fever before all this.

"I...." He still could not look away from Mil, who eyed Mattin like he was a sweet bun filled with cream. "I doubt you kept me waiting long," he finally said.

The previous images—the memories—were blurred and vague until they suddenly weren't. Mattin's spine went straight as a long, deep pull carried through his body, as if his fever had not entirely faded. But then he thought those sorts of memories might have made him feel that way no matter what time of year it was.

"'Ready?'" he asked Arden in a croak. Arden had said he'd made Mattin wait so Arden could ensure he was *ready*. Mattin's face was flaming because he could imagine how Arden would have determined that, and if Mattin had truly been "naked and hungry" in their bed, he would have also been hot, open, and dripping. "I don't like to discuss the specifics, but I should have already been," he whispered it, "*ready*."

He shifted in place, not squirming, although it felt like squirming when his thighs rubbed together, and his cock grew hot and throbbing, and he felt... decidedly used, as if he could feel where Arden and Mil's cocks had been inside him. As if he could still feel where they *weren't*, because he'd been hollowed out and left with a memory that was not enough.

His thighs were, in fact, stinging as if chafed, but also slippery with oil or salve, probably applied by one or both of them at some point to soothe his reddened skin. They might also have given him food or water, although that Mattin did not recall.

He was going to die of embarrassment. He had been unable to care for himself, whining and demanding and apparently scratching them. All the while naked and full of their spend—a great deal of it if they had both repeatedly had him. That was a mess Mattin normally tried to avoid but now he only flushed at the thought and burned while wondering how many times they had taken him in the day or days of his fever. If he had just spread his legs to allow them to rut by the end, if he had moaned for that and they had been indulgent there as well, or if they had been shocked at his wantonness as he continued to make demands and scratch them for responding too slowly.

"You were nearly ready when you got here," Arden explained apologetically, sending a glance to Mil. "But Mil is... large."

Mattin worked his jaw and felt it sore, and looked to Mil as he remembered the stretch of his lips around Mil's cock, then trying his best to get Mil to fuck his throat because he'd been so... *Blessed*. Mil had watched all the while, his gaze almost exactly like it was now.

Mattin made a noise he could not define.

Mil was abruptly serious. "A fever can make you want things that might pain you later. So Arden wanted to be sure, for your sake and for mine. I'd never hurt you, Sass. Not like that."

"I know," Mattin said immediately. "That's why I lov…" He quickly gulped that back down. "That's why I came here. And you didn't. Hurt me, that is. I don't feel more than…" He had no way to describe the sensation of having apparently been filled so well that he still felt it. No way he was willing to tell *them*, anyway. Their expressions if he said he was ruined for any others would haunt him almost as much as knowing it was true, and yet they were going to marry someone else. He forced himself to glance to Arden before facing Mil again. "I'm not in pain."

"That's the funny thing," Mil added, a twinkle in his eye that vanished when Mattin crossed his arms defensively over his chest. "Not that I'm laughing at you, Sass."

"He was laughing at *us* for being surprised." Arden gave Mattin a probing look. "Are you certain you're not in pain?"

"I know what pain is!" Mattin snapped at them without feeling a need to apologize. "And no. Although I am…." He had that sensation again, increasing his desire to shift around and bring his thighs together to better feel where there were no longer any cocks inside him. "I'm…."

The two of them appeared to be hanging off his every word.

Mattin forced himself to be still and hoped they did not look down to the blanket over his lap.

"I can tell I was satisfied," he said primly, putting the twinkle back in Mil's eye and making Arden sigh with pleasure. "You don't need to keep fussing over me."

"He likes fussing over you." Mil snorted. "So do I, for that matter. Thought that at least would be obvious by now."

"He's a little embarrassed, my love," Arden informed his husband. "And perhaps not yet fully aware and awake. Be gentle."

"Gentle?" Mil protested. "I'm the one who got his ass clawed by a wee, sparkly beast!"

"I'm sure I had a reason," Mattin defended himself weakly, not even bothering to be offended about the rest of it.

"You were trying to choke yourself on my cock and I was trying to keep that from happening," Mil answered bluntly, leaving Mattin to contemplate how he had been positioned for that to happen and then precisely what he had been doing to Mil. He sank down against Arden's side before realizing it and trying to pull away.

Arden, who had kept a hold of Mattin's hand, kissed it, stopping Mattin in place. "I think our worry for you outweighed our sense. For that, I am sorry. You are a true Blessed, Mattin Arlylian. You ask for what you can handle and we won't forget again."

"*Ask*." Mil scoffed quietly to himself.

A demand to know what that meant was on Mattin's tongue but he kept it inside. He stared at Arden, not Mil, since for once, Arden was marginally safer to study. Mattin still didn't understand, but if this fever was like his others, he would remember more as he rested and ate. Although he didn't usually allow himself to linger over his fevered actions unless he had done something particularly strenuous and he had to figure out how he'd injured or exhausted himself.

Arden seemed as if he was waiting for Mattin to pepper him with questions.

Mattin dropped his gaze to Arden's other hand, then cleared his throat. "You're reading?"

Arden gave Mattin's knuckles another peck before turning to his reading with a sigh. "I am sorry for this too, dear heart, but as we didn't exactly get to schedule this ahead of time, I still have some things that must be attended to."

"You're the king," Mattin reminded him foolishly.

Arden merely nodded. "But you should eat, and bathe again if you like."

"I bathed before?" Mattin wondered aloud and caught that twinkle in Mil's eye again.

"*He* bathed you. Washed your pretty hair for you too," Mil revealed.

"My very great pleasure," Arden assured Mattin, taking a drink of his own morning tea before looking over his reading once more, which was the list of alliance candidates Mattin had left on the table when he had first... when he had stumbled in here and then apparently crawled naked into their bed and demanded to be fucked. Which they had done, and then cleaned him so he wouldn't return to himself in a sticky, itchy body. That was their soap he smelled on his skin instead of his mint or flowers, and yet he didn't mind it. They had cared for him so well.

"I've never felt good before. After my fevers, I mean." It escaped Mattin with the gentlest sigh. Then Mil was sitting next to him, holding up a pastry for Mattin to take, which he did. "Thank you," he told Mil as well. "I wasn't too demanding, was I? I didn't really scratch you? Not deeply?"

"Want to see?" Mil offered with a proud grin. "You can always look later if you'd like another go. Some do in their waning days, but if you're worn out, that's all right. We can wait. And... we might be a little worn out too. Some of us are not as young as we used to be."

"Slightly younger than me and never lets me forget it," Arden complained mildly. "Eat, dear heart," he ordered without looking up.

Mattin ate, stopping only once he was finished to stare at Arden. "'Dear heart?'"

"You don't care for it?" Arden looked up from the list, a line between his eyes. Perhaps Arden knew some of those nobles already and disagreed with Mattin's choices.

Bright heat flared around Mattin's heart at the idea.

"Seems late to object to the name now," Mil observed, unaware of Mattin's heart and its troubles. "After everything else that was said in our nest."

Our nest. Mattin stared at Mil with wide eyes. "I called it *our* nest? Oh no," he worried with barely a pause, "what else did I say?" It couldn't be worse than the scratching. It couldn't possibly.

"Ah." Arden put the list down again. "Things said in bed, especially in the heat of a lust-fever, might not reflect real desires out of bed. So if you didn't mean it, we won't hold it against you."

"Fuck you, I'll hold it against him," Mil huffed, then deflated. "No, I won't, Sass, I'm sorry."

"What did I say?" Mattin demanded in his rasping voice, then choked when Arden answered.

"That you love us."

Mattin put his head down and accepted the cup of tea Mil hurriedly pressed into his hands mostly because it gave him something to look at.

Arden was being deliberately reasonable. "If you don't, then we should still discuss the matter. Or if, say, you only love Mil, we should discuss that too."

"Why do you keep suggesting that?" Mil snapped at his husband over Mattin's head. "If he's going to fall for just one of us, we both know it'll be you."

"You're better with people, my love, and a hero, and rather handsome, which you know."

"And you're fucking Arden Canamorra and it's a trial every day of my life to not burst with love for you, so quit acting like our Sass couldn't feel the same."

Mattin raised his head. "'Our Sass?'"

The sitting room was silent. Then Arden leaned over and put his lips to Mattin's forehead in a soft kiss. "Yes, if you'll agree, dear heart."

Mattin twisted around to see Mil on his other side peering at him almost anxiously.

"There's already such love between you," Mattin said first, then twisted back around to look at Arden. "You have that list! And an alliance that needs to be made!"

Arden gave Mattin a strange look, a cross between puzzled and amused. "I agreed to consider a political alliance with a suitable beat-of-four of your choosing—" Mattin made a small noise as that was *not* what Arden had agreed to "—because I thought it was wise, and because the country needs peace, and because Mil and I already had our eye on a suitable beat-of-four."

"A pretty thing, despite what he thinks," Mil chimed in. "Bit more used to books than people, or I suspect he'd know that by now. Snippy at times, but in a way that stirs the blood. Smarter than he's got any right to be. And a hungry little Blessed who mewls and begs and demands so sweetly I won't even mind the scars."

"Yet not on this list." Arden looked sad, and it was a trick, it had to be, but Mattin protested anyway.

"Those won't scar," he said of Arden's scratches since he hadn't seen Mil's. "And I'm not on that list because... because..." there was no other way to say it, "you're both heroes, and handsome, and wonderful. I didn't think you'd want.... Arden, I've never even been courted."

"Hmm," Mil interrupted. "You might want to rethink that, Sass. Maybe tomorrow, when your head will be clearer."

"Admittedly, we are older and our methods might be out of fashion. Perhaps I am too much of a Canamorra and act through gestures instead of words." Arden nearly sighed it, as though Mattin wasn't remembering a copy of a copy of a copy of a Canamorra consort at their wedding and the tales of a Canamorra conquering an entire country for them. "Or too subtle," Arden continued, "although if you ask Cael, she will argue we were anything but subtle and I suspect she's right." He hummed, pleased with himself. "Perhaps we should apologize for that, and for possibly scaring off whoever else might have chased after you, but... I don't feel like apologizing for anything today. And if we did scare anyone, it was an accident."

Arden was a tricky liar who didn't do anything accidentally. Mattin didn't call him on it.

"*Oh no.*" Mattin couldn't seem to stop saying it. He started to gesture and Mil had to take the cup from him before he spilled his tea. "That was courting? I thought that was you two being kind about my lonely fevers."

"Mattin," Mil used Mattin's actual name for once, drawing Mattin's attention to him, "courting is about pleasing the other person and giving them things they want or need."

"And spending time with them," Arden added. "Whoever certain nobles thought to have me marry when they suggested an alliance with a beat-of-four, everyone else in the palace knew the most likely candidate was you. Mattin of the Arlylian," Arden pronounced each beat intentionally slow, "you made a charming sight in our nest."

"Be happy to see you return to it when you're in your right mind and freely decide to," Mil continued. "Which could be now or whenever you like. It's your choice, you see. We've made ours."

"*My* choice?" Mattin echoed. He had never dared to imagine any of this and now they were telling him it was up to him? That he could have them in all the ways he hadn't allowed himself to want?

"Tea?" Mil prompted nervously after several moments of Mattin staring blankly at the fire and struggling to breathe normally. "Something to eat? You don't have to decide now. We can try to convince you some more."

Mattin gave up and hid his face against Arden. The towel in his hair impeded him somewhat, so he impatiently tugged it free and tossed it aside. Arden turned to meet him, using one hand to stroke the top of Mattin's spine beneath the curtain of wet hair, soothing all the little stinging places where bruises might show later.

Mattin heard Mil put down the cup of tea, then shift on the seat, so he reached behind him without looking—it was easier without looking—and awkwardly clasped Mil's hand before he pulled it to his chest.

Arden whispered above him, "Flustered, I think." Mil grumbled in reply but let Mattin keep his hand.

"I wasn't too out of control?" Mattin asked, just to be sure.

Mil's breath was warm in more stinging places. "You were perfect."

Flattery. Mattin sighed for it anyway, then raised his head to look at Arden from very close. "I didn't like making that list. I burned the first one."

"We can burn the second too," Arden suggested without hesitation.

Mattin nodded, then dropped his head back to Arden's shoulder. "I can feel... or rather, I *can't* feel, where you were. That is to say, I am empty again." He was so hot. His face, his chest, everywhere. "I think I would like another go," he said next, dizzy for making even an implied demand. "If you don't mind."

"'Mind,' he says," Mil remarked with barely a pause, and tugged his hand free of Mattin's to settle it in Mattin's lap above the blanket. When he realized Mattin was already aroused, he flicked the blanket to the side, then put his hand firmly over Mattin's cock and said, "Ah, Sass," as if breathlessly pleased by how Mattin squirmed against him.

Arden stared down at Mattin's lap and Mattin wanted to squirm for that too, although he was almost afraid to look for himself now that he was nearly feverless. Mil's hand dwarfed his cock, for one. And as for the rest, Mattin imagined his thighs were pink, if not a furious red, and shining with salve. His blood was pounding. Slick welled up inside of him then trickled out, making him shift to get one knee up on the seat so he could get his legs apart. Mil pushed up closer behind him, looming over Mattin in a way that left Mattin shivering with his back against Mil's chest.

Arden watched it all, letting the paper with Mattin's list flutter to the floor somewhere out of sight.

"Are you certain you're not too sore?" he asked while Mil took his hand from Mattin's cock in order to pet the inside of Mattin's thighs. He found what had already leaked from Mattin and made a small noise above Mattin's head.

Mattin hurried to cover himself only to freeze and gaze at Arden with his hand not entirely hiding his stiffening cock from Arden's admiring view.

"Why do you keep insisting I must be sore?" Mattin wondered with less ire than he expected, perhaps because Arden reached down to tug his cock for him, turning as he did so that he could kiss the side of Mattin's neck. Mattin's voice rose on a cry. "Ah, there. I mean... *please*, there."

"Oh, I know you like kisses here." Arden's tone was mean but he kissed Mattin again as Mattin had requested. "You were very clear with your needs, and it was an honor to fulfill them." He raised his head to bring Mil in for a quick kiss, then gave Mattin's neck more attention, kissing a spot that seemed to have been well-loved already, nuzzled often by someone unshaven and a little rough, because Mattin was sensitive there.

His cry grew louder.

"An honor," Arden was a torment, pausing only to run a palm over Mattin's wet thigh before continuing to tease Mattin's cock, "and a joy."

"Please." Mattin had no idea what he was asking for, except, "More."

"More of what?" Mil slipped his hands over Mattin's backside, spreading Mattin wide before sliding his hands between Mattin's thighs again and forcing them apart when Mattin started to wriggle. "Still hot with some fever. Still rubbed raw all over that soft skin from fucking. But you want more." He didn't seem surprised, but he also did not push his fingers where Mattin might have liked them. "Not feverish enough to demand now, Sass? Or is it that you're too sor...?"

"I wear glass. I am not made of it!" Mattin snarled, seizing Arden by the hair and holding him to his neck, only to gasp when Arden—the king himself but every inch a Canamorra—laughed and bit him.

Mil would not let him rub his thighs together. Mil's thumbs swept back and forth over sensitive places, close enough to make more wetness well up and spill. Mattin felt as if he was bright red with heat. "Did you do this to me before?"

"Tease you on purpose?" Mil huffed, moving a thumb to nearly press inside of Mattin. Nearly, but stopping when Mattin whined. "No. A fever's solely about what the Blessed wants. You without a fever... maybe I want to rile you up a bit. See what I can drive you to."

Arden laughed again with warm affection. "Tell him what to do and he will do it," he confided to Mattin in a whisper that Mil could undoubtedly still hear. "Or do nothing and let us show you what you do to us." He used his teeth again and a spasm went through Mattin so strong that Mil had to hold him up.

"Brute," Mattin said anyway, leaving Arden to do as he wanted... and apparently how Mattin wanted. It was not fair how Arden knew what Mattin liked when Mattin did not and couldn't remember.

"Yes," Arden and Mil said together, as they did so many things together, and Mattin abruptly *did* know what they had done, at least some of it. What he had *demanded* they do. What he wanted again now, with his mind clear enough to remember it.

He trembled and flooded an embarrassing amount of slick onto Mil's hands, the spill of it as hot as Mattin was inside. Mil swore. Mattin closed his eyes and fell back against him.

"Gentle brutes," he corrected himself for them, while they bit and groped him and petted over soft, wet skin and kissed him. "Mine." It was a whisper, but they both went still. "My Gifted?"

"Yes," at once and immediate, the two of them speaking as if they knew each other's minds and hearts on the subject and Mattin was the one slow to know the truth.

He was. He blushed for that too, but slid a hand back into Arden's hair and thought of them and understood why he felt marked and carved out inside.

"Then I will have both of you," he continued to whisper, not an order but also not a question, "again. Because we did that, didn't we? In our nest?"

He remained embarrassed but it was difficult to care when they each kissed him; Arden at his neck again, Mil on the top of his head. Mil answered, "'Course we did." But Mattin wasn't sure he understood.

"At the same time," he further explained, as if they were discussing research he had done for them over breakfast and tea. He knew Arden, if not also Mil, were going to worry, and he reveled in that and frowned about it, and added, "It's why I'm so wet now, you see. I've been thinking of it. What I can remember of it. What I can still feel. I was so hungry and then you took care of me. Will you…?"

He had an arm around his waist and was lifted from his seat before he could blink, and raised his voice in startled protest before he could stop himself. Mil froze at the curtains to the bedroom, making all kinds of outraged noises when Arden began to laugh again.

Mattin was held firmly to Mil's chest, his feet dangling without touching the floor. It was not dignified. But something stirred in his chest, and then lower, to know how easily Mil held his weight.

"Do not say sorry," Mattin told Mil. "But you might have chosen a different method to get me there."

"Impatient," Mil answered gruffly, as though he hadn't already had Mattin over the course of at least one day, probably two, possibly three.

Arden appeared next to them to part the curtains and then Mil swooped Mattin into his arms properly to take him into the bedroom.

The bed was bare of many of the blankets, which were puddled on the floor. But Mattin dropped his face to it the moment Mil set him down, rubbing his cheek over the strong scent of his Gifted and the shockingly abundant scent of his slick.

"There he goes again," Mil remarked, hand to the back of Mattin's head as Mattin nuzzled their nest and then turned to roll in it.

Mattin recalled himself a moment too late, already too warm to feel it but aware he must be blushing furiously. The two watching him only seemed pleased. Smug, even, in Arden's case.

"A good nest then." Arden's tone was beyond satisfied. "It will hold that scent for you all of my days, Mattin Arlylian, if you choose us. And you will never be left hungry."

Mattin, on his knees with Mil moving eagerly behind him, blinked several times. "I could never choose anyone else," he answered, because surely that was obvious, and Mil took hold of his thighs, spread them apart, and put his mouth to use.

Hot, Mattin thought in one startled rush of lust and slick. *Mil's mouth was hot.*

When Mattin blinked again, dazed and struggling to get his eyes unstuck, he was on his back on the bed, being thoroughly cleaned of his own spend by Mil's tongue, and Arden was smoothing salve over Mattin's thighs as though Mattin was not soaking the bedding beneath him with steady pulses of Blessed-wet.

"Just trust me, dear heart," Arden murmured when he noticed Mattin watching him, then pulled back, taking a handful of Mil's hair as he did to bring Mil up with him. Mil looked rather glassy-eyed.

"Oh," Mattin realized aloud, almost dreamily, "he will do whatever you say." He understood now.

"And you," Arden informed Mattin with relish, then gently pushed Mil toward the head of the bed. Mattin rolled onto his stomach to watch, his legs splayed quite boldly. Happily, without even a hint of a snarl for Arden directing him, Mil went. He sat with his back to the headboard and his legs out. He was naked, as he had not been when this had started, and his cock was....

"Oh," Mattin said again. He could not remember getting a clear look at it before, but his jaw ached at the sight and his recently spent cock throbbed. Mattin realized he had clamped his thighs together.

They were abruptly but gently eased apart by Arden's big, warm hands.

"Still want us both?" Arden spoke above Mattin's ear, working even more salve over the back of Mattin's thighs, which still tingled from the work of Mil's tongue. Eyes on Mil's cock, Mattin didn't stop him. Perhaps the salve was more necessary than he'd realized. "Mattin?" Arden prompted.

"You are my husbands-to-be," Mattin answered, skin prickling with the sudden return of his fever. "Aren't you?"

"Oh yes." Arden patted the curve of Mattin's ass, abandoning the salve to test Mattin's readiness. Mattin flushed but did not object, only whining softly when Arden slid several fingers in him and spread them wide.

Mil watched them, gaze a little unfocused, and put a hand to his cock.

Mattin had to swallow a sudden flood of spit. Likewise, a gush of wet followed Arden's fingers when Arden momentarily withdrew them. Arden pushed it back into him, giving Mattin's ass a little kiss when Mattin shifted up onto his knees to make it easier for him.

Mattin kept his gaze on Mil and Mil's hand working Mil's cock.

"But you're both so pretty," Mattin remarked, voice hitching.

"Pretty?" Arden carefully withdrew his fingers, then put his slippery hands to Mattin's waist and lifted him. He set him back down in Mil's lap and let Mil keep him upright. Mattin had to stretch to straddle Mil's legs, the salve easing the way only slightly.

Mil was large, and hot, and smelled of nest and Mattin's slick and he held Mattin easily while he positioned him. He filled Mattin a moment after that in one long, smooth push, while Mattin shuddered and tried to be still but couldn't. It didn't hurt but he couldn't breathe with the pressure. Mil's cock seemed to keep going and he would not allow Mattin to squirm. Mattin took, and took, and could not stop a long, desperate moan when Mil was finally deep within him.

"*That* is pretty." Arden said from somewhere behind Mattin.

Mattin, arched and trembling, turned his head to see Arden naked, all dark skin and hair and scars from when he had died. He reached out and Arden came to him, letting Mattin press his hand against his mouth and trying to soothe him with kisses to the top of his head, although he couldn't know why Mattin was upset.

Mil might have, tipping his head up in a way that Arden interpreted as asking for a kiss, which he gave him. Mattin watched closely, and when it was over and Mil's gaze met his, Mattin stretched to kiss Mil too. Arden was theirs and had died. Mil had seen it happen. He should have kisses.

"Beautiful." Arden's hands slid to Mattin's hips as he knelt next to them on the bed. "Look at him, my love." Mil was already looking at Mattin, gripping him tightly and inching up instead of taking him properly. "He doesn't need your care now. Do you, dear heart? You want him to fuck you?"

"Yes." Mattin brought a hand up to pet Mil's mouth, then dropped it to his chest. He started to rock back against Mil's small thrusts, making Mil hiss and grip him tighter.

Arden was as pleased as a Canamorra with a crown in his hands. "Then demand it like the Blessed you are."

Mattin put both hands to Mil's chest and scratched a trail through the hair. "Mil—"

It was all he got out.

Mil moved him as if Mattin was no more than a pillow, fucking into Mattin's slight body by pulling him down, then lifting back up to take his cock again. Mattin was split open, burning inside with slippery heat and friction and outside with distant, already fading embarrassment at the sounds he made and how easily Mil used him.

And Arden watched, stroking his hard cock when Mattin glanced to him, salve on his fingers as if he did not trust Mattin's slick alone for this. But he came forward when Mattin called his name and he guided Mattin's mouth to his cock without being told and held him there, careful but unrelenting. With a groan, Mil stopped thrusting into Mattin. He ground up instead, lighting Mattin's every nerve on fire. Mattin could not suck and moan at the same time, but he tried, failing without concern because Mil did not stop and Arden tangled a hand in his hair and hummed a compliment about his mouth.

Mattin would have kept going, ashamed and thrilled to be ashamed, because he was not lost in a fever, not completely, but he was wild and they didn't care. They liked him this way and wanted to see him even more so.

For that, he eventually stopped, gasping for air and licking his swollen lips and watching Arden with heavy-lidded eyes while Mil teased his cock and pressed insistently inside of him. "Later," Mattin decided in a throaty, husky voice, making Arden's gaze light up. "I want to do *this* again later. But you know what I want now."

Arden nodded. "We do. Lean forward, dear heart, and remember to breathe."

"*Fuck*," Mil said fervently, but took hold of Mattin's thighs.

Arden seemed to take forever to get behind Mattin, and paused once finally there to move Mattin's hair to the side so he could kiss the top of his spine. He put a hand on Mattin's hips and pushed down to hold Mattin still. Mil tightened his grip. Then Arden began to guide the head of his cock into Mattin and Mattin was....

Burning. Not breathing, then breathing in sharply when Mil reminded him, tense with worry.

Mattin had been prepared. His body was still somewhat fever-ready, a faint trickle of slick escaping the tight clutch of his body only to be brushed back over the hot skin by Arden. All the while, Arden did not stop.

Mattin panted, desperately pulling in air now that he'd remembered to, then, all at once, just when it was too much and Mattin nearly cried out for them to stop and his hands tightened and pulled at Mil's chest, he exhaled softly and slowly and deliberately, and he sank into the sensation of *full*, of complete, and tight, and almost, *almost* pain.

"That's it, Mattin-blessed. Dear heart. That's it. Let us in at last." Arden kissed his neck again. Arden kept kissing his neck, breathing hard, his hands clamped down to keep Mattin from moving.

"Fuck, Sass. You feel.... He's not fever-loose, not like—fuck. Sass? You breathing?" Mil was petting Mattin's thighs, anxious and yet still so hard inside him. Both of them were so hard inside him.

"Incredible," Mattin said faintly at last, drawing a small, relieved puff of air from Arden. Mattin opened his eyes, unconcerned with how long they had been closed, to stare at Mil. Mil gazed hotly back at him, biting his lip in his effort not to move.

Mil said, "Arden," in a choked voice. Then, "*Sass*," when Arden urged Mattin in a whisper to kiss him. The kiss was clumsy, open-mouthed, but Mattin didn't mind. Didn't care except to have Mil close and then Arden close too, no longer doubting him. Mil twitched up, just once, jarring Mattin into a groan, and then they were moving, or Mattin was, it didn't matter which. He was aching and full and ruined, bruised very possibly, with how they both held him. He was wet and his thighs burned. He could not take any more and then he could.

"Sass," Mil said again, bright-eyed and pretty.

"More," Mattin answered against his mouth, shuddering as it was given to him.

Mattin was Blessed. He kissed Mil messily and whined high and pleased when Mil reached between them to find his cock. Arden kissed up the side of his neck and down to his shoulder, fingers trailing to where Mattin was stretched until Mattin keened and nearly pleaded for him to stop. but Mattin was on fire as he welcomed them, pained and not-pained, wet and slick and hot because the fae had made him so. They had given him this, he realized, finally understanding why the Blessed were called what they were called.

"An honor," Arden said. a groan between the words, "and a joy."

"Please," Mattin answered, barely able to speak with how full he was. He tipped his head up and closed his eyes to do nothing more than feel his Gifted please him. And they were. *His* Gifted. He allowed himself the growl. "*More.*"

His husbands-to-be obeyed.

The End

The Suitable Verse

Powerful noble families known as the beat-of-fours, answerable only to a ruler and the mysterious, godlike fae, scheme and squabble amongst themselves, and go to war for the chance to put one of their own on the throne. But the fae might be pulling more strings than the nobles realize and they definitely have their favorites.

A series of love stories loosely centered around the political crisis that led to the current ruler, featuring oblivious librarians, crafty though loving kings, an innocent half-fae noble, a legendary outlaw turned conqueror, worried warriors, clever guards, and an infamous beauty.

m/m and m/m/m fantasy romance

A Suitable Consort (For the King and His Husband)

A Suitable Bodyguard

A Suitable Captive

A Suitable Stray (For an Outguard and an Assistant)

A Suitable Brat

Blessed -an alternate universe retelling of A Suitable Consort

Also by R. Cooper

More fantasy and sci fi queer romance:
Fox of Fox Hall
Taji from Beyond the Rings
How to (Not) Train a Firecat
Ravenous
The Devotion of Delflenor
Modern fantasy romance:
The Familiar Spirits Series
The Being(s) in Love Series

About the author

R. Cooper longs to live the life of a fictional 1980s romance novelist (but queer), but, alas, her life is actually mostly spent daydreaming and trying to write, which is at least a little Joan Wilder in spirit, including the crying over manuscripts. R. thought about gender for a while and settled on she/her/they in lieu of anything better, but don't call her a woman because it feels oogie. She lives with her cat in her semi-haunted house somewhere between the redwoods and wine country.

www.riscooper.com

www.ingramcontent.com/pod-product-compliance
Ingram Content Group UK Ltd.
Pitfield, Milton Keynes, MK11 3LW, UK
UKHW020346151125
8985UKWH00009B/833